WHEN
REASON
BREAKS

WHEN REASON BREAKS

CINDY L. RODRIGUEZ

BLOOMSBURY
NEW YORK   LONDON   NEW DELHI   SYDNEY

First published in the United States of America in February 2015
by Bloomsbury Children's Books
www.bloomsbury.com

Bloomsbury is a registered trademark of Bloomsbury Publishing Plc

For information about permission to reproduce selections from this book, write to
Permissions, Bloomsbury Children's Books, 1385 Broadway, New York, New York 10018
Bloomsbury books may be purchased for business or promotional use. For information on bulk
purchases please contact Macmillan Corporate and Premium Sales Department at
specialmarkets@macmillan.com

Library of Congress Cataloging-in-Publication Data
Rodriguez, Cindy L.
When reason breaks / by Cindy L. Rodriguez.
pages   cm
Summary: Elizabeth Davis and Emily Delgado seem to have little in common except Ms. Diaz's
English class and the solace they find in the words of Emily Dickinson, but both are struggling to
cope with monumental secrets and tumultuous emotions that will lead one to attempt suicide.
ISBN 978-1-61963-412-1 (hardcover) • ISBN 978-1-61963-413-8 (e-book)
[1. Emotional problems—Fiction. 2. Family problems—Fiction. 3. High schools—Fiction.
4. Schools—Fiction. 5. Hispanic Americans—Fiction. 6. Goth culture (Subculture)—Fiction.
7. Suicide—Fiction.] I. Title.
PZ7.R618833Whe 2015   [Fic]—dc23   2014009109

Book design by Amanda Bartlett
Typeset by Westchester Book Composition
Printed and bound in the U.S.A. by Thomson-Shore Inc., Dexter, Michigan
2 4 6 8 10 9 7 5 3 1

All papers used by Bloomsbury Publishing, Inc., are natural, recyclable products
made from wood grown in well-managed forests. The manufacturing processes
conform to the environmental regulations of the country of origin.

WHEN
REASON
BREAKS

CHAPTER 1

"When One has given up One's life"

MARCH 7

She lies on the hard ground, breathes deeply, and waits for death to come. She isn't afraid, but anxiety gnaws at her. *Will this take long? Is it going to hurt? What's on the other side? Anything? Will anyone miss me? Or will they be relieved that the miserable girl who screwed everything up is gone?* She takes another deep breath and exhales. *I was broken beyond repair, and they were tired of trying to fix me. They'll definitely be relieved.* Her body starts to relax. Everything will slow down and eventually stop.

Her life doesn't flash before her eyes, like she expected. All she thinks about is this morning. She retraces her steps to make sure everything was executed as she had planned.

She sat in the oversize chair in front of her window, hugging her knees to her chest. The sun gradually broke the darkness and cast its light everywhere. This would be her last sunrise. Wanting to capture it, she closed her eyes and held them for a moment, like she was taking a mental picture, before rising from her chair to get ready.

Like a burglar in her own home, she walked around her room with careful steps and measured movements to retrieve what she needed from closets and drawers. She didn't want to wake or talk to anyone before leaving. She wouldn't have the guts to look her family in the face, lie, and continue with her plan.

Once dressed, she slipped through her partially open bedroom door, with her boots in hand. She stopped in the bathroom, opened the medicine cabinet, and dropped the bottle of sleeping pills into one of her boots.

She paused at the top of the stairs and whispered to those still asleep behind bedroom doors, "I love you. I'm sorry."

Her breath caught in her throat. She swallowed hard, shook her head to stop the tears from coming, and picked up her pace. She practically slid down the stairs and shuffled into the kitchen. After slipping on her boots and coat, she tucked the bottle of pills, the manila envelope, and a bottle of water into her coat pockets. Her note on the whiteboard that hangs on the refrigerator door read: *Mom, I went to school. –E*

She kept her hood up and eyes lowered on the long walk from home to the high school. Outside the building, she checked her watch as students and staff started to arrive for Saturday detention and other weekend events. She had to get in and out quickly. She needed enough time to reach the clearing without getting stopped by anyone.

Hood still up, she entered the school and removed the manila envelope from her coat pocket. She pulled the letter out of the envelope but left the journal inside it. When she reached Ms. Diaz's classroom, she slid both under the door and continued walking. She whispered, "Thanks, Ms. D. You tried."

Once outside, she lowered her hood and took a deep breath. *I'm almost there.* She raised her hood again and ran full speed across the field to the nearby woods.

Now she waits. Her limbs grow heavy and sink into the earth. Her body is downshifting, but her mind is racing. *This is the right thing to do, isn't it? Everything was so screwed up and it was all my fault. The only way to clean up the mess was for me to disappear. And how else can that happen? There was no other way, right?*

But then images of her family and friends flip through her thoughts—stupid stuff—like cosmic bowling and making angels in fresh snow. She pounds the sides of her legs with her fists. "No. No. No," she whispers to herself. She chokes back tears and orders herself, "Do not rethink this." After all, there are far more things she won't miss, like the guilt or the pain. And then she laughs a little, because, really, what could she do now, even if she wanted this to stop?

As her eyelids grow heavy, she blinks hard and forces them open. She squirms on the ground and says, "Don't panic. It's going to be okay," but she can't stop her tears and the choking feeling in her throat. She breathes deeply and, to still her mind, she stares at the sky. Bare branches bump into prickly evergreens as they all sway in the cool wind. They look like they're tickling the blue sky's belly. The sun shines bright and continues its ascent. The moon is visible, but fading. Squirrels race through trees, deftly leaping from branch to branch, and a large black bird, with wings outstretched, glides overhead.

She pounds her fists on the ground and kicks her legs out hard, like she's fighting someone. She rocks her body from side to side and tries to sit up, but fatigue pushes her down. She arches her back and screams and then lies flat. Wanting to hold on to something, she digs her nails into the dirt. Tears slide down the sides of her face as she closes her eyes.

Not far away, Ms. Diaz reads a note slipped under her classroom door, drops everything, and runs as fast as her legs and heart allow. Her legs pump. Her heart pounds. Her arms instinctively clear away branches that threaten to slow her down. A few of the trees' extended branches scratch her cheeks and forehead.

But she won't stop. Her legs and heart pump—fast, faster, go faster, she begs them, until she reaches the clearing.

She pauses for a second, then races to the girl. She bends over her, lifts her body, repeats the word, "No," first softly, then louder until she's screaming. She forces herself to focus, to stop screaming and draw a deep breath. She places her mouth over the girl's and pushes the air in hard, trying desperately to breathe life into her and bring her back.

CHAPTER 2

"Adrift! A little boat adrift!"

EIGHT MONTHS EARLIER, JULY

By 8:30 a.m., Elizabeth figured it was time to get out of bed. She had been up for a while anyway after another restless night. Sleep had been teasing her for about a year, jolting her awake every two hours until she stopped trying, which was usually around 6:00 a.m. It had definitely affected her sunny disposition, or so she'd been told.

She rolled out of bed and shuffled across the hardwood floor to her dresser, where she raked a brush through her jet-black hair. With a section of hair down the front of her face, she resembled the creepy, pale girl from an old horror movie she saw once. Elizabeth tilted her head in a sinister way and snarled. Then she grabbed a pair of nearby scissors and, with one slice, gave herself slightly uneven bangs.

After a scalding hot shower, she dressed and pulled her

hair into a tight ponytail, her newly cut bangs hanging right above her eyebrows. She hastily applied red lipstick and black eyeliner before heading downstairs for breakfast.

Her eleven-year-old sister Lily sat at the kitchen table, watching cartoons and messily eating Cocoa Puffs with a huge spoon. Her mom leaned against a counter, gripping a coffee mug and staring into the space in front of her. Mom was always petite and pretty, but the small lines around her eyes were new. So were the dark circles under her eyes that showed despite layers of cover-up. They had that in common.

"Good morning," said Elizabeth.

"Morning," Lily mumbled through slurps of cereal. She glanced at Elizabeth and then did a double take. "Nice hair," she said and returned to her breakfast and the television. Elizabeth scrunched her eyebrows in response. Was she serious or being sarcastic? If it was a joke, she probably would've gone further, saying something silly like, "Nice hair . . . if you were a gerbil." A genuine compliment? Wow, she wasn't expecting that.

"Morning, sweetie," Mom said absently. Elizabeth stared at her mom, but her gaze went unnoticed. *Hello? Anybody home? Notice anything different, Mom?*

After a few seconds, her mom snapped out of her daze and into action.

"What time is it?"

"Almost nine," Elizabeth said and walked to the refrigerator. As Elizabeth approached, her mom moved away. She tossed a fistful of pills into her mouth and swallowed them with a gulp of coffee before dumping the cup into the sink.

"I hope those are vitamins," said Elizabeth. Mom didn't respond.

"Lily, baby, we need to go. Finish your cereal. We can't be late for camp. I have a job interview this morning, and I want to be on time. No, I want to be early, so there's no chance I'll be late."

Mom was frenzied, clearing dishes, washing her hands, checking her purse for the essentials, and studying herself in the mirror to see if she appeared job-worthy.

"Why do you have an interview?" Lily asked. "You already have a job."

"I know," Mom said as she scanned the room for anything else she needed. "I might get a second job. We need the money."

"Are we really that broke?" asked Elizabeth.

"Yeah, well, I don't want to talk about it," she replied.

"O-kay," Elizabeth said, pronouncing each syllable with sarcastic emphasis.

She waited for a reaction but didn't get one. Mom turned toward Lily, who was still watching TV and slurping her cereal casually.

"Let's go. Let's go. TV off." She hit the power button with one hand and swiped Lily's bowl with the other.

"Mom," Lily whined. "I wasn't done."

"Well, you're done now."

"Why do I have to go to summer camp, anyway? I'm almost twelve."

"Right. In a year."

"I could go to Nana's again."

"You've been going to Nana's since school got out. She deserves a break."

"Then, I could stay with Elizabeth and you'll save money."

"Julia doesn't trust me," Elizabeth said.

Mom was quiet for a second and then said, "We need to go."

As her mother added the bowl to the pile of dishes, Lily inched her way toward the TV.

"Oh, no you don't." Mom stepped between Lily and the television. "I want to get to the interview early, I told you. If we leave in a few minutes I won't have to race around like a crazy person. I want to arrive calm and collected. I don't want to look or feel frazzled."

Elizabeth and Lily caught each other's eyes and stifled laughter. Mom always looked and felt frazzled, no matter how much time she had in the day. While she spun through the room like a hurricane, Elizabeth ate a cold Pop-Tart and washed it down with three gulps of orange juice.

Her mom finally stopped and paid attention to her.

"You should eat a better breakfast," she said.

Elizabeth shrugged.

"Did you get a haircut?"

She nodded.

"When?"

"Recently."

They stared at each other for a few seconds. *Say something. Go ahead, I dare you.*

Mom turned away. Elizabeth watched her cross the room and usher Lily toward the door.

"Later, Lillian Grace," Elizabeth said. Her sister peeked over her shoulder, half smiled, and stuck out her tongue.

"Later, Emily Elizabeth," she responded. "Don't forget to walk your big red dog," she added with a laugh. Elizabeth smiled. Nice one.

Her mom and sister walked out and slammed the front door.

"Good luck, Mom," she said out loud to no one.

CHAPTER 3

"Safe in their Alabaster Chambers –"

An hour later, Elizabeth stood on Tommy Bowles's front porch, jabbing the doorbell repeatedly.

Tommy yanked the door open and ran a hand through his shaggy hair.

"Are you trying to wake up the whole neighborhood?" he asked.

"Just you, Tomás," Elizabeth said, calling him by his proper name. She pushed the bell again.

Tommy rubbed his eyes and yawned. A tall, lanky boy, Tommy wore long khaki shorts and nothing else. His wavy brown hair covered his ears and almost hid his dark-brown eyes entirely.

"You need a haircut," said Elizabeth.

"All things in due time," he said.

"Whatever. Are you inviting me in?"

Tommy stepped aside so she could enter.

"Go put on a shirt," Elizabeth said as she walked into the nearby living room.

"It's going to be like ninety-five degrees today," said Tommy.

"I'm leaving if you're going to parade around half-naked."

"Fine," he said and grinned. He pushed his hands into his pockets, which lowered his shorts enough to reveal the waistband of his boxers. Elizabeth looked around the room as if she hadn't been here a thousand times. "You know, for someone who's so loose about following rules, you really are a prude."

"Shut up and put some clothes on."

"Ah, there's the attitude I love," he said. Elizabeth laughed. As he sprang up the stairs to grab a T-shirt, he shouted, "Hey, check out what's in the kitchen."

Elizabeth moved into the kitchen. Old copies of the school newspaper and shoe boxes filled with pictures covered the table. Among the piles and boxes was a new digital camera.

"Sweet!" she said to herself. She picked it up and started pressing buttons to investigate the features.

When Tommy entered the kitchen—fully dressed—she asked, "Is this for me?"

"Well, it's for the newspaper," he said, joining her at the table.

"So, Mr. News Editor, it's for me. I'm your best photographer."

"True."

Elizabeth returned the camera to its case and opened her messenger bag.

"Sure, go ahead," he said. "Feel free to take the camera and try it out. No need to, you know, ask."

Elizabeth glared at him but couldn't hold it for long.

"I'm going to take the camera and try it out. I'm not asking," she said with a smile.

She rummaged inside her messenger bag, rearranging items to make room for the camera. She pulled out a marble design–covered notebook and moved it to another section of her bag.

"What's that?" Tommy asked.

"Nothing."

Tommy smiled. "Looks like something. So what's in it?"

"None of your business."

"You know, I get all warm and fuzzy inside when we have these heart-to-hearts," he said.

They both laughed.

"What's all this?" Elizabeth said, pointing at the table.

"I'm going through back issues, thinking about how to make the news section better this year." Tommy passed her one of the shoe boxes. "Look, pictures from last year. I found them on the old camera and printed some. Here's one of Nayliz after she got caught in the rain at a football game. Here's Jerel talking to girls instead of selling the paper at lunch."

Elizabeth flipped through a pile of pictures. In a group

shot of the staff, she was crouched down in the front row so that the people behind her weren't blocked. She was smiling, almost laughing. That's probably why her eyes were closed.

In another photo, months later, she's a different person. Her previously chestnut-brown hair—jet-black. Her left eyebrow—newly pierced. Her smile—gone. Her eyes—open, peering into the camera's lens. Her chin—somewhat raised and cocked to the right.

She held the images side by side.

"Have you talked to your dad?" Tommy asked quietly.

"No."

"Maybe you should."

The memory of the last time she saw her father flashed through Elizabeth's mind. She remembered screams, fists, tears, and apologies. She remembered lying on the concrete in the fetal position, begging him to leave her alone.

"That's not going to happen," she said.

"So, you got into a fight. No big deal."

"No big deal? You weren't there."

"What I mean is, it could have been worse. Nobody died."

Elizabeth didn't respond. She thought about her sleepless nights and about her mom—how she stares into space, how they can't have a real conversation. Her stomach clenched, like it did every time her father called the house. Tommy was right. No one died, but something else did that day.

"I'm not going to play 'compare the tragedy,'" she said as she buried the pictures in the box. "I know people are worse off. Still . . ."

Elizabeth stood, sniffed hard, and wiped a tear before it fell. She grabbed her bag and headed for the front door.

Tommy stood and followed her.

"Elizabeth, wait. I'm sorry. I was just . . ."

Elizabeth pulled open the door and raced down the steps. She raised a hand, flashing the peace sign to Tommy without looking back.

Tommy stopped on the porch. He knew better than to chase her. "Okay, then, I'll text you later," he called out, his words bouncing off Elizabeth's back.

Elizabeth alternately jogged and walked until she reached Rogers Park. As she crossed the empty baseball diamond, she unclenched her fists and opened and closed her jaw to relieve the tension. She took a few deep breaths and then let a stream of lukewarm water from an outdoor fountain splash her in the face. She used the bottom of her T-shirt to dry her face, not caring that she was exposing her stomach to anyone who might be looking at her.

Elizabeth removed the camera from her bag and its case and slipped the strap around her neck. As she walked, she paused to take pictures. A child on a swing being pushed by his mother. A babysitter texting on her phone, the little girl she's supposed to be watching pouring a bucket of sand over her head. A lone boy shooting free throws over and over. Elizabeth felt her breath return to normal.

When she reached the town green, Elizabeth cut through the cemetery instead of walking along the sidewalks—a habit that started soon after she moved to town five years ago.

Two months into the sixth grade, she had been playing Frisbee with her dad when she saw Tommy and a woman in the nearby cemetery. Although they went to school together, they hadn't talked much. New to town, Elizabeth wasn't friends with anyone yet. She had left her dad to talk to Tommy.

"What are you doing?" she asked.

Tommy's cheeks reddened and he moved the yellow flowers from hand to hand, like he didn't know what to do with them, like he wished they—and he—didn't exist just then.

"I'm helping my mom. We're putting marigolds on the graves, you know, for *El Día de los Muertos*. She does this every year. We have an altar at home for my *abuela*, but she says we need to honor others, too, even if we didn't know them personally. It shows respect for them and for death. Like, they're gone, but not forgotten."

Elizabeth nodded but didn't say anything. Tommy looked everywhere but at Elizabeth.

"It's kind of weird, I know," he said finally.

"No, it's not. She's keeping them alive in spirit. They'll live forever in a way."

"Yeah," Tommy said. He looked deep into her green eyes and smiled.

Elizabeth had walked over to Mrs. Bowles and said, "Hi.

I'm Elizabeth. I'm kinda friends with Tommy, I guess. I'll help."

"Nice to meet you, Elizabeth. *Gracias*."

"*De nada*," Elizabeth said, pronouncing the words "Day nah-dah."

Mrs. Bowles had smiled wide and handed her a bunch of flowers. She added, "*Dios te bendiga*."

"Okay," Elizabeth had said with a laugh and skipped away.

Since then, Elizabeth and Tommy were best friends and regular visitors to the graveyard. They'd pick up any obvious litter and leave pieces of candy on the square marble slabs. Sometimes they'd read the tombstones and create lives for the dead. All they had were names and dates of birth and death. They filled in the rest.

"Mrs. Lynette Humphrey, a wife and mother to a baby girl who died after a short illness," Elizabeth had said once. "She didn't want any more kids, but she was blessed with three. They all married and made her a grandmother of twelve. She died an old woman, surrounded by her family. She was mostly happy, but her heart was still a little bit broken."

"Mr. John Edward Walters survived the Civil War only to be murdered by Captain Mustard in the Conservatory with the candlestick," said Tommy. "And over here, we have Mrs. John Edward Walters-Mustard who died five years later. Her loving new husband slipped a jar of Grey Poupon into her casket as a reminder of him and their everlasting love."

"Sure, go ahead and make fun of them," Elizabeth said with a smile. "They'll only haunt you as payback. Good luck with that."

One day, while leaving dandelions and Tootsie Rolls on grave sites, they had seen a funeral procession and recognized Sebastiano from school. They didn't know who was in the coffin, but they knew the person must be someone Sebby loved. Tommy and Elizabeth held hands under a weeping willow and observed the ceremony in silence. Shivers shot through Tommy when an older woman's wail pierced the quiet.

"I'm going home," he said. He squeezed her hand, then walked away.

Elizabeth didn't follow him. She lowered herself to the ground and watched the rest of the service. When the mourners left, she placed a dandelion and a Tootsie Roll on the newly dug earth and whispered, "You won't be forgotten."

Unlike Tommy, Elizabeth kept cutting through the graveyard and wondering about its tenants, how they lived and died, but never again in a jokey way.

Elizabeth walked along the grassy rows that separated the tombstones. She stopped at one to straighten an American flag. At another, she lay on her stomach to take a picture of the slim vase with a single long-stem rose.

When she reached the oldest section of the cemetery, she sat cross-legged in front of a weathered gray stone she hadn't noticed before. Her fingertips traced the large letters that told her this was Sophia Holland's final resting place.

BORN ON JUNE 14, 1828
CALLED BACK ON APRIL 29, 1844

"Nice to meet you, Sophia," she said quietly. "You were almost sixteen, just like me."

Her hands shook as she raised the camera to her face.

CHAPTER 4

"The ones that disappeared are back"

AUGUST

Emily had an hour before her best friends came over, which meant she had exactly sixty minutes to clean up and erase her summer. Hiding her journal was number one on her list of things to do. Abby and Sarah would say keeping a journal was childish, and then they'd want to read it. She shoved the notebook with the marble-design cover between the mattress and bedspring, and just in case they got their hands on her phone, she deleted certain pictures and texts. She did the same with her e-mail on the computer.

After she wiped down her dresser, she stopped and studied herself in the mirror. *Would they know? Even with the evidence gone? Would they still be able to tell?* Emily stood straighter and pulled her shoulders back. She circled a piece of hair around her ear and smiled without showing any teeth.

This was her polite smile, the one she had learned from her mom. When Emily was younger, she clopped around in her mom's high heels as her mom made up her face, put jewelry on, and smiled in the mirror. That smile told the world everything was all right, even when it wasn't.

Before heading downstairs, Emily straightened the corkboard on her wall filled with pictures of her, Sarah, and Abby. She touched the edges of her favorite photograph. They were younger, maybe ten. Emily stood between them, her arms wrapped around their shoulders. Abby flashed a peace sign and Sarah leaned her head against Emily's. They all had big smiles, the kind that make your cheeks hurt. She could have told them anything then, back when secrets were fiercely guarded.

Emily hated keeping things from her friends, but she had no choice. The news wouldn't stay here, in her room, shared by only the three of them. A few keystrokes and a "send" button, and everyone would know. And "everyone" would eventually include Emily's dad. When that happened, she'd probably be shipped off to an all-girls private school.

A successful attorney and the town council chairman, Edwin Delgado, lived in the public spotlight, and so did the rest of his family, like it or not. Last year, Emily learned what he meant by "Any slipups will have consequences." The slipup? Emily was featured on the Internet for all the wrong reasons. The consequences? A carefully written formal apology and mandatory volunteer hours at the community health center. She halfheartedly preached about the dangers of teen drinking to delinquents required to be there. Afterward her father warned, "Don't embarrass me again."

"Pop?" Emily called to her dad. He sat in his office, facing the computer, his back to her. He maneuvered the mouse with one hand and held his cell phone to his ear with the other.

He turned the phone away from his mouth and responded, "Yes?," but didn't turn to face her.

"My friends are coming for a sleepover. *Necesito dinero.*" She wasn't sure why she was whispering. It's not like speaking softly would somehow interrupt him less.

He pinned the phone between his ear and shoulder and used his free hand to point to his wallet on a nearby table. She snagged a twenty and returned to the doorway. She wanted to thank him but didn't want to disturb his conversation again. She was about to leave without saying anything.

"Hold on, Luís," her dad said. He put the phone on his desk and swiveled his chair to face her. "I don't recall your asking permission about this. Did you ask your mother?"

"Yes."

"*Está bien,*" he said. "You're staying in the house all night."

It wasn't a question.

"*Sí, señor,*" Emily confirmed.

"No boys or drinking or sneaking out."

"Please, Pop. Do you honestly think we'd do that with both you and Mamá home?" With a smile, she added, "I mean, we might try those things if only Mom were home."

"That's not funny," he snapped. "We're responsible for those girls when they're under our roof."

"Okay, okay. Calm down, Judge Judy."

Her dad smiled a bit. "I'm just saying, sometimes you kids don't think. It's that frontal lobe issue. Did you know your brain's not fully developed, which is why teens are so impulsive?"

"*Gracias*, Dr. Phil. I'll work out my frontal lobe in my spare time; make it nice and developed—buffed, even."

He couldn't help but flash his contagious million-watt smile, the one that helped him to win local elections.

Emily smiled, too.

"Judge Judy and Dr. Phil?" he asked. "You couldn't think of cooler people?"

"They make serious money, Pop. Don't hate."

"Okay then, a television job is now on my bucket list," he said with a laugh. In a stern tone, he added, "Your room should be spotless if you're having company."

"It is," she said and backed out of his office.

On her way to the kitchen, Emily found her mom napping on the sectional in the family room. She snickered because Dr. Phil was on. Emily turned off the TV and put the prescription bottles on the end table into a drawer. Before leaving, she dragged a light cover over her mom and whispered, "Sweet dreams, Mamá."

When the doorbell rang, Emily sprinted to answer it but stopped when she reached the door. Before she let Sarah and Abby back into her life after weeks at camp and vacation abroad, she pulled her shoulders back, circled a piece of hair around her ear, and smiled politely.

CHAPTER 5

"I haven't told my garden yet -"

Hours later, the girls lounged in Emily's room, their bellies full.

"I didn't think both of your parents would be home," said Sarah.

"They won't bother us, though. My dad's working and my mom's sleeping."

"She's sleeping?" asked Abby. "Is she sick?"

"Kind of."

Emily's mom saw a bunch of specialists and had lots of tests done. She swallowed a handful of pills every day. For what? Who knows? The medication made her feel better, but Emily didn't think it was curing anything.

Sarah grabbed Emily's hand and said, "You are in desperate need of a manicure." She retrieved her oversize makeup bag and dug out a hot-pink polish. As Sarah tended to Emily's nails, Abby modeled some of the clothes she bought in Europe. She waved her freshly polished fingers at her friends and said, "I went with my mom yesterday."

"That's nice," Emily said, and she meant it, thinking about her mom passed out on the sofa.

Abby buttoned a pair of red short-shorts and slipped a black shirt with winglike sleeves over her head. "She can be so embarrassing, though. She actually told me she was glad I went to Italy with my aunt, so that she and my dad could have some 'alone time.'" Abby stuck a finger into her mouth like she was forcing herself to vomit.

Sarah laughed but agreed, "That's gross."

Emily's parents never acted like they wanted "alone time."

"And she's always asking me about boys, like I'd ever tell her," Abby continued. She slipped on a pair of black heels. "And speaking of boys. In Italy, they are . . ." She gathered her fingers to her lips, kissed them, and opened them as if she were throwing the kiss into the air ". . . *bellissimo*."

Abby was the first of them to discover boys. Of course, boys had noticed Abby since grade school. She had long brown hair with caramel highlights, blue eyes, and long, lean-muscled legs she showed off whenever she got the chance. When Abby decided in middle school that boys weren't gross anymore, the girls entered a strange new world—ready or not. Sarah was ready. Emily was not.

It's not that she didn't notice boys. She had crushes and flirted. In eighth grade, she even dated a few guys, but she broke up with each of them pretty quickly. Whenever Sarah or Abby nudged her to take the next step, she panicked and ended it, saying he was too short, too tall, too geeky, or too dumb. Really, she was scared.

She didn't want to be publicly dumped like Nicole Taylor was in the seventh grade. Anthony Ramos walked the entire length of the cafeteria one day and announced that Kent Miller was done with her. Nicole tried to act nonchalant, but she started to cry when Kent high-fived Anthony. No thanks. Getting dumped after opening your heart was bad enough, but then she'd have to relive the experience over and over once people posted and shared the pictures or videos, adding comments along the way.

And all of that would sooner or later be seen by Luís the tech-geek college student hired to answer phones, make copies, and scour the Internet for any mention of the Delgados, in particular her dad's cases and local politics. That's how she got into trouble last year.

Emily tried to stay on the romantic sidelines and cheer her friends on, but they always pulled her into the game.

"Remember when we tried hooking you up with Ben last year?" asked Sarah.

"Yeah, what a disaster," said Emily.

"It didn't have to be. He called you every day," said Abby.

"And I didn't know what to say. He talked a lot. I listened. He asked questions. I answered."

"Awk-ward," sang Sarah.

"Exactly."

Emily wanted Ben to leave her alone, but when he did, she was surprised. When two days passed without a call or text, she played it off like she was relieved. She never admitted to her friends how conflicted she was.

"I still don't know what the problem was," Abby said. "Ben really liked you."

"I guess, but he wasn't 'The One.'"

"Why did he have to be 'The One'? And anyway, how do you know? You didn't even give him a chance. He could have been your Romeo."

"I don't want a Romeo," said Emily.

"Every girl wants a Romeo," Abby snapped.

"Romeo was in love with someone else and forgot all about her when he saw Juliet."

"That other girl should have tried harder. You should have tried harder."

They were all quiet for a minute. A conversation with Abby was often like living through a minor earthquake. It was too small to register on the Richter scale, but it definitely caused some damage.

"She tried with Kevin," offered Sarah, who always tried to salvage whatever cracked during the tremor.

Abby smiled and put on a pair of large sunglasses. Emily giggled. If Abby tried to walk in heels and sunglasses, she'd probably land on her face. Emily secretly hoped it would happen.

"Yeah, so what about Kevin?" asked Abby. "Did you hear from him this summer?"

Abby pulled her sunglasses down her nose to get a good look at Emily.

"No."

Abby held Emily's gaze for a moment, then pushed up her glasses and said, "That's too bad."

"Yeah, I guess."

Emily focused on Sarah as she applied another coat of polish, but her mind was on that party in June, the last big one before freshman year ended.

Sarah and Abby had pulled Emily into this group-dance thing that was more like drunken swaying. Abby had kept nudging her toward Kevin. When Emily was close enough, he had wrapped his arms around her waist.

Emily glanced over her shoulder, where Abby smiled and gave her the thumbs-up sign. Emily looked down and shifted from side to side. She focused on the music and tried to ignore Kevin's hand stroking the center of her back.

Dizzy from the beer and the hot air in the cramped basement and the fact that his body was pressed up against hers, Emily had tried to pull it together. She clutched his shoulders to steady herself, and Kevin responded by tightening his grip around her waist. His hips moved against hers. She followed his lead. Emily buried her flushed face in his shoulder, and he slowly steered them away from the group to an open spot by a wall.

"Are you okay?" he asked.

"I'm just hot," she said and fanned herself with both hands.

"Don't move." While he was gone, she remembered to

breathe. He returned with a cup of beer. She drank half of it in a few swallows. He smiled and leaned into her, his mouth next to her ear. She inhaled sharply and then let the breath out steadily when her lungs started to burn.

"Is it true?" he had asked. He smelled pungent and sweet at the same time, a combination of cologne mixed with sweat.

"What?"

"That you've never been kissed—really kissed?" Emily's stomach muscles tightened. Abby and Sarah were the only people who knew this, or so she thought.

Almost everyone had some experience, even if they hadn't gone all the way yet. She had avoided it all, but now she was embarrassed by her never-been-kissed status. She saw Abby and Sarah across the room, whispering and pointing in an oh-my-god sort of way. She looked down again and nodded.

"I think that's sweet." He rubbed the tip of his nose over her cheek. Her whole body clenched and started to tingle. With his forefinger, he lifted her chin. She didn't pull away. His soft lips pressed against hers. His tongue parted her lips, and they kissed, really kissed, for what seemed like forever but was actually only a few seconds.

When they stopped, he asked, "Do you want to get out of here?" Emily shook her head, no. Her heart pounded, revealing the truth. He smiled faintly, grabbed her hand, and led her back to the party.

The guys exchanged fist-bumps while Sarah and Abby encircled Emily and pelted her with questions. As they moved away from the boys, Abby said, "Hold on." She ran back to

Kevin, grabbed his hand, and tugged him toward her. She whispered something in his ear and squeezed his hand.

"What was that?" asked Emily.

"Nothing," Abby had said. But Emily knew it was something.

"Hey, Abby, what did you say to Kevin that night?" she asked.

"I don't remember," Abby said, waving her hand.

"It's too bad that didn't go anywhere," Sarah said and blew again on Emily's nails.

"Yeah, well, I wasn't surprised. I mean, the picture Abby took of us ended up all over the Internet and that troll Luís sent it to my dad."

They all laughed hard.

"It wasn't funny." Emily wiped a tear that seemed to be from laughter.

"I'm sorry, but Prince Harry got naked in Vegas and he's still royalty," said Abby. "They didn't, like, demote him, or anything. Your dad is a town councilman, not the president. Come on, you're going to kiss people and have a couple of drinks. He needs to get a grip."

"My dad's a *lawyer* and the council *chairman*," said Emily. "We were drinking *illegally* in someone's house when they were out of town. Plus, we were supposed to be at the movies before crashing at your house. If you want to try to convince him all of that is totally normal, I'll get him now."

"Uh, no thanks. I don't want to be cross-examined. Sounds painful," Abby said, and they all laughed again. Abby was done showing off her new clothes, so she changed into pajama pants and a tank top and joined them on the bed. "I'm so sorry about what happened with your dad. I still feel like a jerk for posting that picture, but I was so excited for you and it just happened. I really wasn't thinking."

"Wasn't the first time and won't be the last," added Sarah.

"Hey," Abby said and slapped Sarah lightly on the leg.

Emily settled into the pillow behind her and smiled, picturing the three of them much younger, with pigtails and missing front teeth. The dynamics were the same, though. Abby had always acted like the big sister, leading them along like she knew the way and being blunt "for their own good." She always said, "Best friends say something when you have lipstick on your teeth. I'm not going to let you walk around looking or acting stupid." Sarah was like the eye-rolling middle sister who always put Abby in her place and made Emily feel better. They fought sometimes, like sisters do, but they always protected each other. At least, they used to.

"Seriously, Em. I'm sorry about the picture. I've bought you like a hundred pints of coconut ice cream since then to make up for it."

Emily put a hand on her belly and grunted, "Ugh, no more, please."

"And don't worry about getting into trouble," added Abby. "We'll be super careful from now on—stealthy like ninjas."

"Exactly," Emily said with a smirk.

"So it didn't work out with Kevin. Oh well, time to move on," said Abby. "He's hot, but he's a dog. He's dated most of the sophomore class by now. You know, he had sex with a high school girl when he was in eighth grade."

"*If* the rumors are true," said Sarah.

"They're always true," said Abby.

"Whatever," Emily said, stopping the exchange. "Let's talk about something else."

Emily's phone buzzed. She checked it carefully so she wouldn't mess up her nails. She read the text and tucked the phone into her front pocket.

"And who was that?" Abby asked, raising an eyebrow.

"Nobody. I mean, my brother Austin. He's bragging again about being in college."

"Speaking of hot boys," said Abby.

"Now, *that's* gross. We are definitely not talking about my brother."

"Then let's move on to hair and makeup," Sarah suggested. Sarah was already picture-perfect. Her black, tight curls hung loose, and her face was lightly made up so that her dark-brown skin, tinged red from days on the beach, seemed to glow. Emily would be the guinea pig.

"Sure. I'll be right back."

In the bathroom, Emily pulled out her phone and read the text again. She smiled wide and typed a quick response. Then, she deleted the thread. *Why didn't she tell them?* They asked about him and she lied. It was the perfect time to tell them. Maybe it's not too late. She could do it now, but they'd have to promise no posts or tweets or texts to anyone. She looked at herself in the mirror. What was she going to do?

Ask them to pinkie swear? That was kid stuff. Even if they did it for old time's sake and a good laugh, it wouldn't stick.

She had no choice but to keep the secret and lie to her friends as long as she could. They'd want to know *everything*, and they couldn't help but spread the news. And when any of the news reached her super-conservative dad, she'd be grilled as if she were a criminal on the stand. And no one, not even Mamá, would object to protect her. Emily gripped the edge of the counter and squeezed her eyes shut. She drenched a towel with cold water and pressed it against her face. The few tears she couldn't hold back soaked into the cloth.

"A clean canvas," Emily said pointing to her face when she returned. She nearly fell asleep as Sarah brushed her thick hair this way and that. When Sarah moved to Emily's face, she pressed her thumbs into the flesh beneath Emily's eyes.

"You're a little puffy," she said and cocked her head.

Emily shrugged. "I probably need more sleep."

Sarah studied Emily for a moment but didn't push the issue. "No problem," she said. "I have just the thing." Her hands moved deftly across Emily's skin. She mumbled as she worked.

"This goes perfectly with your brown eyes and dark, auburn-tinted hair . . . This will fill out that thin upper lip to match your plump lower one . . ." When Sarah finished she said, "You are done, and you are gorgeous."

Emily closed her eyes and felt her face redden.

CHAPTER 6

My Letter to the World

MARCH 7

Dear Ms. Diaz,

Hi. How are you?

Okay, that was a stupid way to start, but I wasn't sure how to begin. Deep breath and here goes: When you read this, I should be gone. The first envelope is my suicide note, and this journal is the explanation. "This is my letter to the World / That never wrote to Me —" That's a line from an Emily Dickinson poem, but I'm sure you know that. Do you know how that feels? To expect a response from someone and get nothing? She was ignored and resented it. So was I. Not by you. You tried. I didn't make it easy, I know. I never made things easy. Like Emily Dickinson, I hid myself away from the world. I was there, but I wasn't—not really. Does that make sense? I wanted people to notice me, the real me, but I didn't let anyone see me.

I'm sure people will be surprised by what I did. They'll find my notebooks in my locker and rip my life apart, page by page, to find answers to their questions. Even then, they might not understand. I wanted to tell you myself. It wasn't an impulsive decision. People might think so because of what happened yesterday. That's not the reason why, but it was the last straw. I'm not blaming anyone else, though.

I'm the one who let it all get to me. Some people can shrug things off. Not me. I mulled things over and over until they were a part of me. I saw and felt things differently than they did. Kind of like Emily Dickinson. Turns out, we shared a lot more than our initials.

You know, once, she said her father's "heart was pure and terrible." And she said, "I never had a mother. I suppose a mother is one to whom you hurry when you are troubled." These lines could've been from my own journal, but they were written by someone born almost two hundred years ago. Weird, right? I mean, we felt exactly the same about certain things, like how we wanted to be remembered in the end.

That same poem about her writing a letter and never getting a response? Well, she does get noticed. At the end of the poem. And after her death. The last line of that poem is a request. I ask the same of you, Ms. Diaz.

Please, "Judge tenderly – of Me."

CHAPTER 7

"Denial – is the only fact"

SEPTEMBER

Emily walked alone to the bus stop at the corner of her street, her earbuds firmly in place. Others also blocked out the world as they waited, but a few huddled together and talked. Sue Huntington, a freshman, chatted with three boys. She caught Emily's gaze and waved. Emily circled a piece of hair around her ear and spun her small pearl earring. She smiled politely and waved back but didn't join the conversation. Instead, she turned her attention to her iPod and searched for a better song. While she waited, she kicked small loose stones or texted Sarah and Abby, who were already on the bus.

She acted like she wasn't concerned about anything, but she was. Emily had come close to telling her friends, but she didn't. The last thing she wanted was to start the year with the kind of drama that put her at center stage. Been there. Done that.

After that June party, when she and Kevin had kissed in the corner in front of everybody, her phone blew up with texts, posts, and tweets. She had played it perfectly—not too modest, not too confident—and had basked in the warm glow of the spotlight.

Kevin turned up the heat with some flirty posts. Emily's body tingled with nervous excitement in response to each one. Things were different this time. She wouldn't pull back like she did in middle school. She wanted things to move forward.

But then her dad saw the picture. The giddiness inside her evaporated and was replaced by humiliation as her dad berated her about her lousy judgment and loose morals— *¡Qué vergüenza!* In normal families, the scolding would have been followed by a month-long grounding. Case closed. But Councilman Edwin Delgado, Esq. had crafted a lengthy letter to the editor that was published in the local newspaper. In it, Emily apologized and her dad promised to address this serious problem both in his home and the town he loves and serves. Emily's public shaming at the health center had followed.

When the bus rounded the corner, Emily pulled her shirt down and smoothed the front of it. She wanted to tell her friends, but she couldn't. Not yet. The spotlight would find her again and she didn't want to get scorched.

The bus hissed to a stop. Emily hung back and let everyone

else climb on ahead of her. Once she got to the top step, Abby and Sarah stood up and screamed her name. They waved her over and hugged her when she reached the seat, as if they hadn't seen her in years. Emily laughed and shushed them at the same time. People rolled their eyes at the dramatic welcome.

"Oh please," said Abby. "They're just jealous because no one is jumping up and down to see them."

"We are a little loud," Sarah admitted and giggled. "Oh, well."

Two stops later, Elizabeth Davis waited in line to board the bus. Emily inspected her through the window. She was tall and had an athletic upper body. Her thick, straight hair was pulled tight into a ponytail.

When Elizabeth climbed on the bus, Emily got a better look at her: uneven bangs, black eye makeup, and light-green eyes. An eyebrow piercing, big black hoop earrings, and a pouty mouth painted deep purple. Emily remembered how different Elizabeth looked when she moved to town. Emily secretly gave Elizabeth props for having the guts to reject the school's unofficial head-to-toe designer clothes dress code. She was bold, which made Emily nervous, but she was also, in her own way, beautiful.

Elizabeth caught Emily staring twice. The first time, Elizabeth let it go. The second time, they locked gazes and Elizabeth flipped her off. Abby and Sarah were talking, so they didn't see it. Emily joined their conversation to avoid Elizabeth's glare as she passed the group to find a seat in the back.

When the bus arrived at the front doors of the high school, Sarah said to Emily, "Wait a minute." She reached into her backpack and retrieved a small tube of pink lip gloss.

"Hold still," Sarah said. Emily parted her lips a little as Sarah applied the gloss.

"There," she said when she was done. "Now, you are absolutely perfect. Watch out, boys."

"Yeah, right," Emily said.

"Keep it. It's too light for my skin tone. Be sure to reapply throughout the day. It really calls attention to those gorgeous lips. Plus, it tastes like bubble gum."

Emily smiled and shook her head as she slid the lip gloss into her pocket.

They filed off the bus and marched into the packed main hallway. Kevin Wen-Massey leaned against a wall, talking with Tommy Bowles. When the girls entered the building, Kevin said, "There she is."

"Good luck, man," said Tommy. "I'll see you in first period. I'm going to find Elizabeth before class."

"Of course you are. Give her a kiss for me, okay?"

"Shut up." Tommy punched Kevin lightly on the arm before he walked away.

Kevin cut a path to the girls. His blond hair was carefully styled to look windswept. He wore an oversize T-shirt and barely-held-up baggy jeans.

"Well, hello, ladies," he said once he was in front of them.

"Hi, Kevin," Sarah and Abby responded in unison and laughed. Emily didn't say anything, but she laughed, too.

"Come on, hugs all around," said Kevin, holding his arms open to Abby. As he hugged her, he said, "You're looking gorgeous as usual."

"Thanks," Abby responded. "How was your summer?"

"Excellent. Went on a cruise with my dads and hung out here." He moved down the line. "Sarah. How was your summer, beautiful?"

"Great," she said, tapping his back as they hugged. "Camp. Beach. Lots of shopping."

"Awesome." He stepped to the left and stood in front of Emily.

"Hey." Kevin wrapped his arms around her and held her for a moment. Sarah and Abby raised their eyebrows at Emily as she peered over Kevin's shoulder. This was no quick pat on the back. They would definitely be talking about this later.

When they separated, Kevin asked, "So, how was your summer, Delgado?"

"It was okay," she said with a shrug.

"Just okay?"

"Well, yeah, my friends were gone most of the time," she said, motioning to Abby and Sarah.

Kevin grinned mischievously at Emily. Suddenly nervous that he would say something more, Emily announced, "I'm going to find my locker before class. I'll see you in first period."

As Emily weaved through the halls, Kevin followed her at a safe enough distance not to appear suspicious.

Emily stopped in front of her locker and fumbled through the combination. Kevin arrived a few seconds later and leaned on the locker next to hers. She glanced at him and acted disinterested.

"So, your summer was just okay, Delgado? Really?"

Emily nodded and choked back a laugh.

"Damn, that's harsh. Couldn't you have said it was good, at least? I mean that's better than okay—not by much, but better."

"It was good," she admitted. Emily cracked a smile and continued to put a few things into her locker.

"If you were being honest, then you would say it was great."

"Let's not get carried away," she said jokingly.

"Oh, really?" He leaned over so that his mouth was near her ear. "Maybe you need a reminder," he whispered.

"*¡Basta!*" Emily snapped.

"That is so hot," he said and inched closer to her.

Emily backed away and looked around. Satisfied that no one was paying attention to them, she said in a clear, low voice. "Kevin, we talked about this. You know I haven't told Sarah and Abby. I'm sure they're going to ask me about the hug, and I'll have to convince them it meant nothing. I swear, I'll disown you if you tell anyone or make it obvious."

"All right," he said. "Chill. I get it." After a few moments of silence, he added, "I'm going to walk away. Wait a few seconds and then follow me."

"Where are you going?"

"You'll see," he said before he left.

Emily closed her locker and spent the next few seconds zipping her backpack and adjusting the straps so that it hung exactly the right way. She glanced down the hallway to see where Kevin was and then began to follow him.

Both said hello to friends along the way, but they kept moving. Kevin led her far away from the main hallway and down a flight of stairs. He crossed an empty corridor, opened a door, and went in. Emily looked around. The coast was clear. She opened the door hesitantly and stepped inside the dark room.

Kevin grabbed her and lifted her in a hug. Emily let out a little scream and then laughed.

"For someone who doesn't want to attract attention, you sure make a lot of noise," Kevin said as he put her down.

"It's too dark in here to see you," Emily said. "What is this place?"

Kevin pulled out his cell phone and turned on the flashlight function. He waved the light around so Emily could see the room. Costumes hung on rolling clothes racks, and small props cluttered most of the room. One table held several wigs and cases filled with makeup, the thick kind that won't melt off the actors' faces under the glaring lights.

Emily stared at a large sketch of the tragedy and comedy masks that covered one wall. The weeping Tragedy seemed both frightened and sorrowful, while the laughing Comedy was oddly sinister.

"It's a storage room," Kevin said. "I discovered it last year when I dated Thalia, the drama queen."

"Don't be mean."

"No, I'm serious. She starred in almost every show, so I called her my drama queen. Not in a bad way, like a nickname," he explained.

"Cute." Emily crossed her arms in front of her chest and turned away a little. She grabbed her small silver crucifix pendant and pulled it back and forth along her thin necklace.

"Thanks," he said. "Let's not talk about her."

Kevin left the flashlight function on and set his phone on a nearby table. "It's not candlelight, but . . ." They stared at each other for a few moments. "Come here."

Emily let her backpack slip off her shoulders. She walked slowly to Kevin. When she reached him, she slid her hands around him, locking her fingers across the small of his back.

"Go ahead," she said. "Remind me."

Kevin didn't hesitate. He lifted her face and leaned down to kiss her. Emily closed her eyes and pulled him so close there was no room for worry or fear. The rest of the world melted away. His kiss on her neck and his hand through her hair were the only things that mattered, the only things she needed or wanted.

When they stopped kissing, he whispered, "You taste so good."

"It's bubble gum," she said and giggled.

The bell rang.

"That's the first bell," he said. "We have time."

"Not enough," she said.

"Says who?"

They laughed.

"Kevin, we are in *school*," she said. "I don't want to get suspended on the first day."

"A suspension on day one would be bad, but then everyone would know. No more worrying about when or how or if to tell them. Problem solved, right?"

"Not exactly." Emily gently pushed herself away from him and stepped back. She grabbed her backpack and slung one strap over her shoulder. "You don't get it."

"I get it. Everyone will talk about us for a few days, and then something else will happen, and we'll become old news. I give us a week, two tops, and then nobody will care."

"I don't know," she said. "I mean, that picture of us was everywhere and my dad was so mad. Madder than I've ever seen him."

"But wasn't your dad more concerned about the beer in your hand than the kiss?"

"Trust me, my dad cared about the kiss *and* the beer. My point is, it was all public. I was embarrassed and had to do that ridiculous community service and I was grounded forever. If everyone knew we were together after that . . ."

Kevin moved close to her and cupped one side of her face in his hand. He stroked her cheek with his thumb.

"They'd what? Think you were stupid? So what? I've been called a lot worse. Who cares, Em?"

"I do," she said and pulled away from him. "Abby and Sarah are my best friends, but they can't keep things quiet. And everything I do gets back to my dad, like it or not. I'm part of a family that's in the public spotlight. I hate it, but I can't do anything about it, except keep a low profile."

Kevin shook his head.

"We've got to go," she said.

"Fine." Kevin grabbed his cell phone and aimed the light at the door. "You go first."

Emily opened the door and peeked out to see if anyone was in the hallway. Before she walked through, Kevin said, "I'll see you in first period, but don't worry. I'll act like I don't know you."

She stared at him for a second, but didn't say anything. She wondered if it really had to be all or nothing. If it did, then which would be worse: being exposed again or being ignored? She couldn't decide. She turned away from him and smoothed the front of her shirt with both hands. She looked out the door one more time before she left.

When she reached the upstairs main hallway, she slipped into the noisy crowd and headed to her first period English class. As she walked, she pressed a palm to her flushed cheek and then swiped her fingertips over her bare lips. Before entering her class, she pulled out the pink lip gloss from her pocket and smeared on a fresh layer.

CHAPTER 8

"We introduce ourselves"

Elizabeth could peg a teacher within twenty minutes, and she gave them one class period to amuse or impress her. If they did, then she'd engage. If they didn't, she'd do barely enough to get by. If they weren't going to try, why should she?

As she approached her period one English class, Elizabeth saw Ms. Diaz standing near the door with a welcoming grin on her face. Elizabeth tried to speed through the doorway, with Tommy close behind her, but Ms. Diaz jabbed something into Elizabeth's elbow. Stunned, Elizabeth turned, her eyes wide and her hand clenching the strap of her messenger bag that cut across the front of her body.

"Sorry, but you'll need one of these," said Ms. Diaz. She handed Elizabeth a bookmark that read: "Dwell in Possibility –" Emily Dickinson #657.

Elizabeth crossed the room to join Kevin, who sat near the windows. She slid into a desk in front of him, and Tommy sat on her other side.

"What's up, Davis?"

"Hey, Kev," said Elizabeth.

"I told Tommy to kiss you for me. Did he?"

"Dude . . . ," Tommy started.

"Obviously not or he'd be in the nurse's office right now," said Elizabeth.

"So, I see summer didn't melt the Ice Queen," Kevin said and laughed.

"Shut it, Kev, or I'll shut it for you." Elizabeth sat back and scanned the room.

On the largest wall, a poster of Shakespeare hung to the left. His large, pale forehead stood out against his dark, curly hair and the poster's deep-red background. His lips smirked beneath his moustache, and his brown eyes glanced casually to the left, like he just told a dirty joke.

To the right was a black-and-white poster of Henry David Thoreau. He wore a black suit jacket and a bow tie just below his wide-collared white shirt that was buttoned high up the neck. His scruffy half beard and mussed-up hair contradicted the outfit, which was way too uptight for someone who was a tree-hugging rule breaker.

Between these men sat Emily Dickinson, straight and tall in a chair, her right arm gently resting on a nearby table, her left hand holding a flower, a violet maybe. She wore a dark dress with a high, scooped neck, topped with a tiny row of white lace. It had long sleeves and pleats across the top and throughout the waist. Around her neck was a black ribbon edged in white, buttoned at the nape. Her dark hair was parted down the middle and pulled back tight. She stared straight ahead with her serious, dark, penetrating eyes. Her round cheeks led to full, unsmiling lips. Her pale, porcelain-like skin seemed to glow against the darkness that surrounded her.

After everyone arrived, Ms. Diaz started to seat her students in alphabetical order. No surprises there. Granted, it was probably the easiest way for teachers to learn their names, but still. Elizabeth had been sandwiched between the same students for years. She had never been friends with either of her D-named neighbors, and considering the exchange she had with one of them on the bus, she wasn't looking forward to what was coming.

"Tomás Bowles," Ms. Diaz started.

"Here," he answered and moved to the seat nearest the door.

"Interesting combination."

"My mom's Mexican, my dad's English-Irish," he explained. "You can call me Tommy. My mom hates that, by the way."

Ms. Diaz smiled and made a note on her roster. "I'll be sure to use 'Tomás' during parent conferences."

Elizabeth took a good look at Ms. Diaz: tanned skin and black hair that was parted down the middle and fell below her shoulders in loose curls, almond-shaped, dark-brown eyes, and a full mouth painted deep red. She was petite and slim, but she had curves. She wore a knee-length black skirt, no stockings, a business-casual purple shirt with three-quarter sleeves, and black shoes with three-inch squared heels.

She was put together and cared about making a good first impression, knowing it could stick for the rest of the year. She also moved and spoke with confidence. Students are like dogs; they'd take over if they sensed the slightest bit of fear. Elizabeth knew Ms. Diaz wasn't a first-year teacher, which was a good thing. Elizabeth hated first-year teachers.

After a few more names, Ms. Diaz called, "Emily Davis and Emily Delgado."

Emily Delgado moved first. Elizabeth stayed seated near the window and watched as Emily pried herself away from her friends to take her seat.

Elizabeth snarled at Emily in her creepy-horror-chick way. Emily shifted her gaze and stared at the top of her desk.

"Emily Davis?" Ms. Diaz called again.

"Since we look so much alike, you can call me by my middle name, to avoid any confusion," Elizabeth said as she walked to her new seat.

"Which is?"

"Elizabeth."

"Okay then, Elizabeth," Ms. Diaz said in a pleasant tone while changing the name on her roster. "Do you prefer Liz or Lizzie or Beth or anything like that?"

"No," she responded curtly.

"So, Elizabeth?"

"Yes, ma'am," she confirmed and saluted Ms. Diaz with two fingers.

Tommy smirked, all too familiar with Elizabeth's rough edges. Kevin smiled and saluted her back. Elizabeth nodded but kept a straight face. She folded her hands Catholic-school style, but her knuckles faced the front of the room and her palms opened toward her.

Ms. Diaz scribbled something down. Elizabeth was sure it was more than a name change. She would love to read all of the side notes written about her since last year.

Once all of the students were seated, Ms. Diaz began with the basics: expectations for behavior, her grading policy, and the year's curriculum. She explained that they'd often read, analyze, and write poetry to cultivate their creativity and encourage them to consider the power of words.

"Because in poetry—more so than other genres—every word matters," Ms. Diaz said. At this point, she seemed lost in thought and emotion. She talked about the power of words and the importance of being a great communicator in an increasingly competitive world that ruthlessly splits people up based on education levels.

"Even if we set aside the importance of mastering words for our futures, think about how words affect us each day in different ways. A note or comment from a friend can make us feel better or infuriate us. Dialogue in a movie can make us laugh or cry. And music . . . How many of you play a song over and over?"

Hands shot up. Ms. Diaz walked around the room. Elizabeth held one hand in the air and scribbled in her notebook with the other. She covered the pages with her forearm when Ms. Diaz walked by.

"Why do we play a song repeatedly?" She didn't wait for an answer. "Because it speaks to us in some way. The words hit us here," she pointed to her heart, "and here," she pointed to her head. "That doesn't happen in math class," she said with a smile.

Students laughed.

"Don't tell your math teachers," she added with another smile. "My point is words are powerful. We will read them, explore them, use them wisely, and use them wildly. We can disagree with each other, but everyone's ideas will be considered. We can analyze, even criticize, one another's comments and work, but choose your words carefully. Words can uplift and they can wound. I do not want anybody wounded here."

Elizabeth raised her eyebrows. She never figured someone might get hurt in an English class. Woodshop, yeah. Science, maybe. But English? Still, one thing was clear to Elizabeth: Ms. Diaz loves this stuff.

She was impressed.

Of course, not everyone would be.

"Are we going to have to write one of those what-I-did-on-my-summer-vacation essays?" Kevin asked.

Ms. Diaz stopped in front of his desk and stared at him for a second, purposely creating an uncomfortable silence.

Elizabeth predicted her teacher's response: *Kevin, didn't you hear a word I said? Do you really think someone who worships language would ask you to waste words on an essay about the countless hours you played video games?*

"No," said Ms. Diaz.

"Really?" he said. "Cool. I always thought those were dumb."

"Dumb?" she asked. "An essay is neither dull witted nor unable to speak."

"Huh?" he asked.

Elizabeth laughed.

"I think you mean 'pointless,' " Ms. Diaz suggested.

"Sure. Pointless."

"I agree."

"Really? Cool."

"Very," she said. "Instead, let's get right into a bit of literary analysis."

"Ugh," Kevin responded. "Not cool."

"Sorry," Ms. Diaz said with a smile and then walked to the front of the classroom.

Elizabeth was amused.

"Take a look at the bookmark I gave you," she said, holding one in the air. "It's the first line of an Emily Dickinson poem. She's one of my favorites, so we'll read several of her poems this year. The whole first line is 'I dwell in Possibility.' On a sheet of paper, I want you to respond to the first line as best you can."

"Can we read the rest of the poem?" Elizabeth asked without raising her hand.

"Not today. You may ask questions or predict what the rest of the poem may be about. You may apply it to yourself. What are your possibilities as you begin the year? I want to see what you can do with a limited number of words and limited time because, as of right now"—she paused and glanced at the clock—"you have only twenty minutes."

Students groaned.

"Let's get started," she said.

Elizabeth watched as her teacher's words sparked a flutter of activity. Students opened binders, tore out pieces of paper, and dug in bags for pens and pencils. Some students, like Emily Delgado, were walking supply stores; others, like Kevin, would be lucky to find a pencil in their pocket. Some students got right to work, writing down the phrase and whatever came to mind. Others stared at the bookmark like deer caught in headlights. Ms. Diaz circled the room to save the clueless ones.

Elizabeth didn't need any help. Her left arm circled her paper like she was guarding a government secret—head bent low, hair cascading from her ponytail over the sides of her face. Her hand moved frantically.

When she stopped for a quick break, Elizabeth eyed her neighbor. Emily sat upright with her legs crossed under the desk; she held the corner of the paper with her left hand and wrote neatly with her right. She stopped and tapped her pen against her cheek, like this would incite further inspiration, and then returned to writing.

Twenty minutes later, Ms. Diaz announced, "It's time to

hand in whatever you have. Don't worry if it's incomplete. I don't expect a masterpiece."

"Is this going to be graded?" Kevin asked.

"No," she said after another uncomfortable silence. "It's a snapshot of how you think under pressure. It's a place to start."

"Oh, good," Kevin said, relief in his voice. "See you tomorrow, Ms. D," he added as he handed his paper to her.

"See you tomorrow," she responded.

Ms. Diaz stood at the door, just inside the classroom, so her students could pile their papers on her hands as they left. Elizabeth scanned the room. Some students left the bookmarks on their desks. A few were on the floor. She tucked hers into her messenger bag.

She reviewed her work before handing it in. Across the top of the page, she wrote, "Words can wound," surrounded by tiny daggers dripping with blood. Beneath this, she sketched a house with the word "possibility" across the front door. A girl stood inside, looking out a window covered with prison bars.

On the back, Elizabeth wrote: "dwell—to inhabit, have as your home. To dwell in possibility: to live in possibility. I think the quote is meant to be optimistic. Make possibilities your home; live out the possibilities.

"But, the quote can be pessimistic, too. To dwell on something means to never get past it. If you dwell in possibility, you might not accomplish much. Like the guy who has million-dollar ideas but stays poor his whole life. Possibilities are great, but you have to take action. If you get too comfortable in your home of possibilities, then your dwelling becomes a prison before you realize it. Your home becomes a jail that sucks the life out of you."

She underlined the last sentence twice.

Elizabeth smirked as she placed her work on top of the others.

"Have a great rest of the day," Ms. Diaz chirped.

Elizabeth nodded. *You impressed me* and *you amused me. Let's see how you handle this.*

CHAPTER 9

"Forbidden Fruit
a flavor has"

Emily entered Kevin's house through a sliding glass door he always left unlocked for her and stepped into the bathroom off the kitchen before heading upstairs. While applying a light layer of pink lip gloss and a thin line of light-brown eyeliner, she grinned, thinking about the first time she stood in this bathroom.

It was mid-July, and Emily was thankful that Sarah and Abby had left town for their summer vacations. Yes, they were her closest friends for as long as she could remember, but she had needed a break. Sarah and Abby had refused to be wallflower ninth-graders who inched their way into popularity. Instead, they all parachuted into the thick of things, a triple-person jump with Abby pulling the cord. Emily had no choice but to hit the ground running. Sometimes she felt like a fraud because, truth was, half the time she would have been happy staying home. Other times, she had kept pace with her friends but was always worried about getting caught doing something wrong. And then she did get caught.

Emily and her brother Austin had started working in Pop's office when school got out, which wasn't so bad in the beginning. They even rented a booth at the town's annual summer festival, where Emily painted kids' faces and Mamá sold her perfectly seasoned empanadas to support the Little League team that Pop sponsors. Austin didn't do much. He called it working the crowd, but Emily called it flirting. Pop shook a lot of hands and gave free legal advice. At one point, Emily thought she had seen actual tears in Pop's eyes as he looked from one family member to the other, watching them work together. *Of course he was happy*, she thought. *This was all for him.*

Unlike Emily, her brother was actually interested in the law, which meant he often joined Pop on his trips to court and left her alone in the office with Luís, the tech-geek-spy, of all people. His apologetic speeches about how he was only doing his job were met with Emily's death stare and polite smile. To avoid Luís, Emily texted Abby and Sarah. They tried to make her laugh about the situation, which didn't really help. When they left town, Emily was left with an overly chatty Luís, a pile of unsharpened pencils, and Candy Crush.

So, when Kevin had texted her one Saturday afternoon with an invitation to swim at his house, she jumped out of bed and jammed a swimsuit and change of clothes into her backpack. Austin gave her a ride. She had easily lied to him and her parents, saying lots of kids would be hanging out.

When she arrived, Kevin was in the back, already in the pool. He smiled wide when she walked through the gate. He pushed himself out of the pool in one fluid motion and walked to her, dripping wet. When he reached her, he hugged her tight and kissed her temple.

"I'm glad you're here," he whispered. Butterflies tap-danced from the top of her throat to the bottom of her stomach. He led her by the hand into the house and to the bathroom. "Meet me outside," he said.

After changing, she covered her stomach with one hand and her mouth with the other. She quietly screamed with excitement and nervousness and then lowered her hand to breathe deeply and calm herself.

She had briefly questioned herself: *After everything that happened, what are you doing here?* But she laughed because the answer was obvious. She wanted to be here. And she wasn't doing this because Abby or Sarah pushed her into it, or because her dad pulled her away from it. This was her choice. She took one last deep breath, walked outside, and dived in.

She had returned every chance she'd gotten since then. Keeping him a secret made everything sweeter somehow, but now Abby and Sarah were back and school had started. Things would be more complicated.

Emily set aside her concerns as she climbed the stairs and walked into Kevin's room. From the doorway she watched him sleep for a while and then crawled onto the bed beside him. She rested her head on his shoulder and draped her arm across his chest. She closed her eyes, exhaled, and let herself sink into the mattress.

He felt her and curled his arm around her shoulder, pulling her closer to him.

"Hey," he said and kissed the top of her head.

She lifted herself to kiss him on the lips.

"I love your lip gloss," he said and then gently pulled on her bottom lip.

He leaned back and they lay quietly for a while, holding each other.

"I was thinking about the first time I was here," Emily said. "Why did you invite me that day?"

"Because I wanted to."

"Was I the only girl not away on vacation? I mean, if Sarah was in town, would you have texted her instead?"

"Believe it or not, I don't ask out every girl who crosses my path," Kevin said. "I asked you. I didn't think you'd say yes, but I asked anyway."

"Why did you think I'd say no?"

"Because you're usually glued to Sarah and Abby, and I had already tainted your spotless reputation. After all the publicity, I figured you'd tell me to go to hell."

Kevin laughed. Emily turned and propped herself on her elbow. He swiveled, too, so that they lay side by side.

"But here you are." He reached out and held her free hand. "So, tell me, why did you say yes?"

"Because I wanted to." She smiled. "If it was anyone else, I would have said no."

Kevin smiled wide and squeezed her hand.

"Being with you *here* is easy," she said. "At parties, I feel like everyone's watching and commenting . . ." She shook her head and stayed quiet for a while. "You know what I like best?"

"I know," he said and raised his eyebrows. "I can tell."

Emily pulled her hand free and hit him on the shoulder.

"I like to watch you sleep," she said. "And I like when you hold me and whisper things like, 'Are you okay?' or 'Are you comfortable?'"

"Yeah?"

"Yeah."

Kevin held Emily closer and then rolled on top of her. She shifted so that her legs were on either side of him. As they kissed, Emily slid her hands under his T-shirt and rubbed his skin. Kevin moved back and pulled his shirt off. He grabbed Emily's hands and gently tugged her so they were both kneeling on the bed. She rested her hands on his hips while he buried his in her hair at the base of her neck.

"So, what do you want to do now?" he asked and smiled.

"Let's go swimming," Emily said and moved off the bed.

"What?"

Emily laughed as she reached for her backpack. "You're closing the pool soon, so we should take advantage of it."

Kevin, still kneeling on the bed, stared at her in disbelief.

She walked to him, kissed him on the cheek, and whispered, "We don't only have to swim."

Kevin laughed and Emily left to change in the bathroom.

Emily beat Kevin to the pool and lounged on a chair while she waited for him. As he came toward her, he said, "You're not afraid someone will see us out here? Abby and Sarah might be in the bushes with binoculars and cameras, taking pictures and posting them all over the Internet. Maybe the local paparazzi were tipped off. You know, they've already nicknamed us EmKev or is it Kevily?"

"That's not funny," said Emily.

"It might be safer to stay in my room," he said and wiggled his eyebrows.

Emily tilted her head and grinned but didn't say anything.

"Seriously, though, I know we kind of talked about this yesterday, but I really want to know how long this whole secret-boyfriend thing is going to last."

"You're in my sun," she said and motioned for him to move.

He smiled, raised his hands, and backed away a few feet. He crossed his arms and waited for a response.

"I don't know," she said. "You said it yourself: my reputation will be ruined even more."

"I was joking."

"But it's true." Emily stood up. "Everyone will have something to say, and I really don't want to hear it. I don't want to feel like I have to defend myself because I'm not ashamed of being with you."

"You shouldn't be. We haven't done anything wrong."

"I know."

"So, what's the problem?"

"Well, let's see . . . Sarah and Abby will be pissed when they find out I lied. And even if they're not, they'll talk about our every move." Emily paced while she talked. "And then my dad will find out—*por supuesto*—and force me to talk to middle schoolers about abstinence or something. *¡Ay, mátame ahora!* And, what if, while all of this craziness is going on, something happens between us?" Emily lowered her gaze.

Kevin put his hands on Emily's shoulders. "Jeez, *chica*, you are tense." He turned Emily around and massaged her upper back. "Now let me give you some 'what ifs.' What if your friends are just happy for us? What if you tell your dad to back off and let you live your life?"

Emily shook her head. Kevin turned her around and lifted her chin with his finger.

"What if you trust me when I say I won't hurt you? And what if you stop worrying about everything and enjoy the moment?"

Emily's stomach tightened. She hugged him, resting her head on his shoulder. Could it really be that easy? Thinking about the aftermath of the June party, she doubted it. She'd never seen her father so angry. She'd never been more upset with Sarah and Abby for not understanding the position she was in, for thinking her problems could be solved with another manicure or pint of ice cream. But, they did promise to be more careful. Maybe, with her friends protecting her, and Kevin by her side, everything could be different this time. Still, right now, while their relationship was a secret, she had him, her friends, and no family drama.

"I don't want to tell anyone yet," she said, looking up at him. "I want to keep you to myself for a little while longer. Is that okay?"

"I'll take what I can get," he said and grinned. "But I'm not going to do this forever, Em. I don't like to play games."

Emily nodded.

Kevin started to fuss with her silver cross pendant, moving the clasp to the back.

"Wait," she said and touched his hand. "You're supposed to make a wish when they touch."

"Okay," he said with a laugh. "Make a wish."

She closed her eyes and let Kevin fix her necklace. When she opened them, he was gone. She turned her head and saw the tail end of his cannonball into the pool.

Emily patted her pendant and repeated her wish before she jumped into the water.

CHAPTER 10

"I dwell in Possibility –"

Elizabeth stormed into the classroom seconds before the bell. She dropped her bag to the floor as she plopped into her assigned seat. Her hair was down, hanging straight. She wore black jeans and high-top Converse sneakers, and an oversize army-green T-shirt tied in a knot in the back. Even stretched as it was, an outlined sketch of Frida Kahlo could be seen on the front.

"Okay class, let's begin," Ms. Diaz said after the bell. "I read your first-day reactions last night."

Elizabeth had been digging through her bag but stopped to listen to her teacher.

"Very interesting," Ms. Diaz said.

What the hell was that supposed to mean? Elizabeth's response was genuine. She didn't draw and write what she did to provoke her teacher, but it wasn't typical. And all she gets in return is "Very interesting?"

Elizabeth was not impressed.

Maybe she was wrong about Ms. Diaz.

She pulled a beat-up copy of *Wuthering Heights* from her bag. She slouched in her seat and rested the opened book in the space between her body and the edge of the desk.

"I love seeing the variety of interpretations," Ms. Diaz continued.

Unlike yesterday, Elizabeth only half listened. She scanned the room and noted Tommy whispering to Abby about how he grows out his hair in the summer and then shaves it off in the winter during swim season. Abby listened intently while she circled one of his wavy strands around her finger. Tommy grinned and blushed but didn't pull away. *Stupid seating arrangement.*

Given their last names, Elizabeth would have been looking at the back of Tommy's head if they had been seated in normal rows. But, no, Ms. Diaz put them in a double semicircle to "encourage discussion." *Bad move and good luck keeping our attention.* Even worse, because of this fancy seating arrangement, Elizabeth had a clear shot of Abby and Tommy. Elizabeth finger-combed her hair forward to try to block them from view.

"As readers, you'll bring your own experiences to your literary interpretations," Ms. Diaz continued. "So, each of us can see something different."

After several more glances at Tommy and Abby, Elizabeth

forced her attention elsewhere. Next to her, Emily sat up straight, books and notebooks neatly stacked on her desk. She was mouthing a question to Sarah across the room, using her hands in a form of sign language they seemed to understand. Kevin, who sat behind Sarah, witnessed the exchange and joined in. He made exaggerated, nonsensical signs to imitate the girls, which made Emily and Sarah giggle.

"I'll pass back what you wrote yesterday," Ms. Diaz said. "We'll read the rest of the poem and analyze it a bit. And then for homework, you'll write a one-page, typed reaction to it, building on what you started yesterday. This will be due the day after tomorrow."

Students groaned. Elizabeth agreed. She was not amused.

"This isn't a research project," Ms. Diaz added. "I want a one-page paper, no more, so you shouldn't need more than two days."

"Wow, Miss," said Kevin. "You don't mess around. We have a paper due the first week of school? What about a get-to-know-you activity?"

Elizabeth laughed along with the rest of the class.

"First, please call me Ms. Diaz." She walked around and distributed the students' first-day papers, a copy of the Dickinson poem, and the directions for their assignment. "Second, you're a sophomore in high school. The days of the week-long, get-to-know-each-other, lovey-dovey stuff are over."

"Aw, man," said Kevin.

Ms. Diaz placed Emily's papers on her desk. Elizabeth watched the girl immediately pick them up and read them.

She opened her school-issued agenda to write down the assignment.

Elizabeth glanced at her paper. "See me at the end of class" was written on the top. She smirked, turned the essay over, and returned to her book.

"Third," Ms. Diaz continued, "getting right to work is the best way to transition out of summer vacation and into school. Trust me. I'll go easy on you today."

"Okay, okay," Kevin said.

Ms. Diaz returned to the front of the room. "First, let's talk briefly about Emily Dickinson. Does anyone know anything about her?"

"She was a poet," said Kevin.

"Yes, thank you for stating the obvious," Ms. Diaz said with laughter in her voice. "Anyone else?"

"Didn't she live around here?" asked Abby.

"Yes. She lived in Amherst, Massachusetts, which isn't far from here. Anyone else?"

"She was a recluse," said Elizabeth. She closed the book but was still slouching.

"True," said Ms. Diaz. "At about the age of thirty, Dickinson retreated from society, staying mostly in and around her home."

"Why?" asked Tommy.

"Good question. No one knows for sure. Some of the theories are: an illness, depression, a broken heart, maybe. She may have simply chosen to live a quiet life and dedicate her time to her work. She wrote almost eighteen hundred poems, but according to the Emily Dickinson Museum, only ten were published in her lifetime and likely without her knowledge."

"Should we be writing this down?" Kevin asked, interrupting her.

"Yes," said Ms. Diaz. "You can assume that anything we discuss may come back to haunt you on a quiz."

Elizabeth rummaged through her bag and retrieved a notebook and pen. Kevin had nothing but a single-subject notebook on his desk. He patted his pockets but came up empty. He leaned forward and gently scratched Sarah on the middle of her back with his finger to get her attention. Sarah wiggled a little at his touch and turned to hear his request for a pen or pencil.

Elizabeth noted how Emily crossed her arms as she watched the exchange. When Kevin saw Emily looking in his direction, he winked at her, but she looked away quickly. Elizabeth would ask him about it later. On the other side of the room, Abby now sat sideways so her perfectly tanned legs directly faced Tommy. Elizabeth sighed and continued to stroke her hair forward to block them out. *Worst seating arrangement ever.*

"Dickinson's poems were discovered and published after she died, and she has since been considered one of the most important American poets in history," said Ms. Diaz. "I'll tell you more about her as we read her poems throughout the year. Let's get to today's selection."

Ms. Diaz projected the first stanza of poem #657 on a

wall. She asked Emily to read aloud. She seemed startled to be called upon but didn't protest. She read:

I dwell in Possibility –
A fairer House than Prose –
More numerous of Windows –
Superior – for Doors –

"You were supposed to go easy on us. This is making my head hurt," said Kevin.

"Good," responded Ms. Diaz. "That means you're thinking. Now, who can tell me what's going on in the first stanza?"

No hands went up. Elizabeth stared at the lines of poetry, rereading them several times. She then started to write and draw in her notebook.

"What do you notice about the poem? Let's start there."

Tommy tentatively raised his hand. Ms. Diaz nodded at him.

"She uses capitalization in unusual ways."

"Good. That's a start." Ms. Diaz underlined the capitalized words.

"Should we be underlining these?" asked Kevin.

"Yes," she said. "Now, what does the capitalization do for these words?"

"Gives them importance," said Tommy.

Abby smiled admiringly at Tommy. Elizabeth noticed when she peeked from behind her hair-curtain.

"Good," said Ms. Diaz. "Please read the rest of it, Emily."

Elizabeth raised her gaze from her notebook to the projected poem. Emily sat up straighter and read with a clear, singsong voice:

Of Chambers as the Cedars –
Impregnable of Eye –
And for an Everlasting Roof
The Gambrels of the Sky –

Of Visitors – the fairest –
For Occupation – This –
The spreading wide my narrow Hands
To gather Paradise –

Ms. Diaz waited to let the words settle. "So, what is she talking about?"

"I have *no* idea," Kevin said. Several students giggled, but not Elizabeth. She lowered her head, letting it hover a few inches above her work. She furiously jotted notes and drew.

"Anyone else?" Ms. Diaz asked. "Is anyone else confused?"

Several hands shot up. Elizabeth didn't raise hers.

"That's all right," Ms. Diaz said. "Dickinson is often hard to understand. Let's take a closer look. She says she dwells in Possibility, and then she mentions Chambers, Gambrels, and Visitors."

"She's describing it like a house," said Sarah.

"Yes, good. Now, what is she describing like a house? Where does she dwell? Where does she live?"

"In Possibility," said Tommy.

"Yes, but what is Possibility? What does it represent?"

The class was silent for a while. Some students stared at the poem, others at their desks, hoping not to have their names called.

"Poetry," said Elizabeth.

"What was that?" Ms. Diaz asked, a little surprised.

"Poetry," Elizabeth said louder. "She's talking about poetry. She doesn't go out usually, so she lives through her poetry."

"Why do you think that?"

"Partly because of what you said about her. Writing is what she does. It's her Occupation—capital 'O.' Also, because she compares it to prose. Writing is either prose or poetry, so she's talking about poetry. She thinks poetry is better, a fairer house; it allows her to better capture what she sees, the paradise that surrounds her."

The students stared at Elizabeth and Ms. Diaz, waiting for a response.

"I'm impressed," said Ms. Diaz.

Elizabeth wanted to smile but didn't let herself.

Several students scribbled rapidly into their notebooks.

"Wait, can you say that again?" asked Kevin.

"No, no," Ms. Diaz said. "I don't want your papers to be about what Elizabeth thinks. I want to know what each of you thinks. On one of your handouts, I was kind enough to list some websites to help you analyze the poem. The one-page response must have some analysis, but the main question is personal: Where do *you* dwell?

"As Elizabeth said, Dickinson lived through poetry; it's the vehicle through which she observed the world and expressed herself. So I want to know: What is your vehicle? How do you express yourself? We all have something that helps us to make sense of this world.

"Use the rest of the class time to start the paper. Some of you can use the computers to check out the websites. I'll walk around to help anyone who needs it. Let's get started."

For about twenty minutes, Ms. Diaz circled the room, answering questions and reading students' developing work. When the bell rang, students packed up and filed out the door. Elizabeth lingered, obeying the note on the paper handed back to her.

"You wanted to see me?" Elizabeth asked.

"Yes." Ms. Diaz smiled and sat on top of a desk. "It's about your paper yesterday."

Elizabeth stared at the floor. Her heart started to beat faster.

"You're obviously very smart and creative," she said, tilting her head down. Elizabeth realized Ms. Diaz was straining to establish eye contact, so she looked up. "Your comments today and the detail in your drawing yesterday were both impressive. I talked with Ms. Gilbert yesterday . . ."

Elizabeth blinked hard and clenched her jaw.

"You're sending me to guidance?"

"No. Don't worry, you're not in trouble," said Ms. Diaz. "She told me how you often draw within your notes, that it's a way for you to capture what's going on in class and in your mind. That's fine, but if you draw weapons like the bloody daggers yesterday, then I have to report it. I think you know that. I want to encourage your creativity, but we do have school rules to follow."

"Got it," said Elizabeth.

"Do you have any questions?"

"Nope."

"Okay, then." Ms. Diaz scribbled on a piece of paper. "Here's a pass to class. See you tomorrow."

Elizabeth grabbed the pass, and as she strolled down the hallway, she crushed it in her fist.

CHAPTER 11

"Afraid! Of whom am I afraid?"

Later, Emily skipped lunch, telling Abby and Sarah she had to meet with her counselor to change a class. Instead, she sneaked out a side door and tucked herself into a corner near the art wing, far enough from the cafeteria that her friends shouldn't find her.

Sitting on the grass, her knees pulled up to her chest, Emily's heart pounded as she texted Kevin. She retyped the message a dozen times before she settled on: It's over.

Her phone buzzed seconds later.

Kevin: WTF? Is this a joke?

Emily: No.

Kevin: Meet me in the drama storage room. Let's talk.

Emily: I can't.

Kevin: I deserve an explanation.

Emily: Fine. I'm outside, near the art wing, by the bench-sculpture thing.

Kevin: On my way.

Emily stood and paced. Her hands turned cold, but her heart pounded. She sat on the bench-sculpture, ignoring the sign telling students not to, leaned forward, and gripped the seat so hard her fingers hurt. She wanted to appear calm when Kevin arrived, but she couldn't stop her legs from bouncing.

Kevin rounded the corner in a jog. Emily remained seated.

"What's going on?" he shouted.

She sprang to her feet. "Be quiet," she said and looked around.

"No one's here but us."

Kevin closed the gap between them and instinctively reached for her.

"Don't touch me," she warned.

"What's wrong?"

"Yesterday, we made out in the storage room and hung out at your house."

"Right."

"You said you wouldn't hurt me."

"Yeah, and?"

"You did."

"How? What did I do?"

"You scratched Sarah's back in English class this morning," said Emily.

Kevin's eyes widened in surprise and then scrunched in confusion. Finally, he laughed.

"You're joking, right?"

Emily's entire body clenched.

Kevin stopped laughing. "Wait, you're serious."

"You were flirting with her."

"I just needed a pencil."

Emily held her hand up to stop him from talking.

"I know I'm not your official girlfriend, that we had decided to keep everything a secret—"

"*You* decided," he interrupted.

"Forget it," Emily said and started to rush past him. Kevin grabbed her elbow to stop her.

She yanked herself free. "I said don't touch me."

Kevin held his hands up. "Whoa, easy. I'm sorry. I'll let you talk."

Emily zipped her silver crucifix back and forth along the chain until her breathing slowed. She patted the small cross and continued.

"You're right. I decided to keep us a secret. You wanted to tell everyone. You said you wouldn't wait long, and then you flirted with one of my best friends in front of my face. You say you were asking for a pencil. I say you were sending me a clear message, a warning even, that if I didn't tell everyone about us, you'd move on, with Sarah."

Kevin opened his mouth to defend himself, but Emily held her hand up again.

"I actually felt sick to my stomach, you know that? The thought of you being with Sarah after being with me—I wanted to puke right there all over my desk."

Emily started to pace.

"What was I thinking? *Yo estoy tan estúpida.* I avoided all this for as long as I could and then I gave in completely, with *you* of all people! A Romeo who was kissing me one minute and scratching Juliet's back the next."

She stopped pacing and buried her face in her hands.

"What are you talking about?" Kevin asked. "Listen, I SparkNoted *Romeo and Juliet* last year, so if you're going to bring Shakespeare into this, you have to fill me in."

Emily dropped her hands and returned to the bench-sculpture. She reclined, resting her head on the hard edge and looking up at the sky.

Kevin stood in front of her. "So, what do you want to do?"

"I want to rewind time. I want to go back to the way things were . . . before . . ."

"Yeah, well, good luck with that. You can't erase what happened, Emily, and I don't understand why you'd want to." He smiled at her and moved his hands up and down along the front of his body, as if to say, *Who would want to forget all this?*

"Anyway, I thought you said you weren't ashamed to be with me," he added.

Emily didn't crack a smile. Her eyes remained fixed on the streaky clouds above.

"I'm not. I don't mean you. I mean way before you, when things weren't so complicated," she said.

"I don't see how things are complicated. We like each other and we're together now. So what? It's not like you're dating Mr. Jordan. Now, that would be bad because he's old and gross, and well, it's a crime, so he'd be in jail and the story definitely would be all over the news. It'd go national if you were pregnant with his baby. Compared to that, our story is pretty straightforward and actually kind of boring, don't you think?"

Emily sat up straight and tried to think. She bent her head from side to side and rubbed a painful knot in her neck. "This isn't funny. You don't get it. I kept us a big secret and then lied to my friends. If I tell them now, they'll be upset."

"They'll get over it," said Kevin.

"Probably, but when my dad finds out I have a boyfriend, I'm dead."

"Wait, first you said this was about me flirting with Sarah, then it was about keeping secrets from your friends, and now it's about your dad? Which is it? You know what, don't answer. They're all shitty excuses. You are way overreacting here."

"Maybe, but what am I supposed to do?"

Kevin held his hand out. She reached for it, and he tugged her to her feet. Unsteady as she stood, Emily grasped his hands.

"Listen, Em, I'm sorry about the Sarah thing. These hands will never touch her again," he said, holding them up. "And breaking up doesn't solve anything, unless you plan not to date anyone ever again. You'll have to face your friends and family sooner or later, Em. Face them now, with me."

Tears streamed down Emily's face.

Kevin pulled her into a hug and held her tight.

"Don't cry," he whispered.

Emily balled her fists against Kevin's back. Her body convulsed as she sobbed and took in everything about him: his scent, his strong arms and chest, how their bodies seemed made for each other, the way they interlocked perfectly. *Why couldn't she just let this happen? Let herself be happy with Kevin? Let herself forget about what everyone else thinks?* When she regained control, she pulled away. Kevin wiped her face with his hands and kissed both of her cheeks, her eyelids, and her forehead. Finally, he kissed her softly on the lips.

"Okay," she whispered.

"Okay? Really?" Kevin grinned.

"Really, as long as . . ."

Kevin interrupted her with his famous from-the-belly yell he uses to get the crowd going at basketball games. He hugged her tight again and shouted, "Emily Delgado is my girlfriend, everyone! That's right, the two hottest people in this school are off the market!"

Emily playfully shoved him.

"I was about to say as long as we keep things quiet. Not secret anymore, but you know, quiet, the opposite of yelling," she said while laughing. "We can't make out in the halls or go anywhere near the drama storage room or get caught drinking at any more parties."

"Whoa, you didn't mention all these boring rules before," he said with a laugh.

She moved closer and wrapped her arms around his waist.

"It won't be boring, but I can't do anything that will light my dad's fuse. Promise me we'll keep what we do as private as possible."

"I promise," he said. Kevin began to fuss with her necklace, moving the clasp to the back like he did the day before. "Make a wish," he whispered. Emily put her hand behind Kevin's neck and pulled him to her. The world seemed to disappear while they kissed, but then they heard a familiar voice.

"Gotcha!" Abby said, holding up her smartphone.

Emily covered her mouth and bolted, leaving Kevin behind, holding the small silver crucifix in his hand.

CHAPTER 12

"A Secret told –"

Kevin shouted, "Abby, knock it off!" and Sarah yelled, "Emily, wait!" But she didn't.

Emily bolted through the door and hustled down the hallway to the nearest girls' bathroom. She lowered her head as she entered, not wanting anyone to notice her red, puffy eyes. Two girls she didn't recognize passed her on their way out. They were too involved in their conversation to notice her.

Alone in the bathroom, Emily rushed into the last stall and locked herself in. She dropped to her knees, pulled her hair back, and leaned over the bowl. Her stomach was tight and that seasick sensation floated in her head. She breathed deeply and allowed her muscles to relax. She started to feel better and knew nothing would come up.

She slipped her backpack off her shoulders and placed it

on the ground. She sat on top of it, pressing her back against the wall, and started to cry again. When the door creaked, Emily tried to stifle her sobs.

"Are you okay in there?" the girl asked. "Not that I care, really."

Emily didn't answer. The girl walked into the neighboring stall and said, "I'm going to stand on the toilet and peek over the top of the stall. I'm warning you in case, you know, you're not decent."

Emily didn't respond.

"All right, then, I'm going to assume you're dressed and all."

The girl climbed on the toilet rim, curled her fingers over the top of the stall, and popped her head over.

"Are you okay?" Elizabeth asked.

Emily ripped off some toilet paper and dabbed her eyes.

"I'm fine," she said.

"You don't seem fine. I can go get someone, or I could stay here with you if you want me to. I don't mind skipping a class or two."

Emily smiled a little. Everyone knew Elizabeth was familiar with the detention room.

"No, thanks. I want to be alone."

"Are you sure?" asked Elizabeth. "Once I told someone to leave me alone, when really I wanted him to stay."

The girls stared at each other for a moment.

"Do you really want me to leave you alone?" asked Elizabeth.

Emily wanted her to stay more than anything, but how could she spill everything to Elizabeth—a girl who flipped her off on the bus and never talked to her?

"I'm fine. Leave me alone."

"Okay," Elizabeth said. She stepped down off the toilet and left the stall. When she got close to the door, she said, "I'm leaving now," as if to give Emily another chance.

Emily squeezed her eyes shut and covered her mouth with both hands. Several minutes after Elizabeth left, the door opened again.

"Emily? Are you in here?" called Sarah. "Come out, come out wherever you are."

Emily stayed quiet.

"Olly olly oxen free," Abby added.

The phrase triggered memories of hide-and-seek, lemon-ade stands, and running through sprinklers, which made Emily smile a little. She stood, opened the stall door, and walked toward her friends.

"I'm here," she said quietly.

Sarah and Abby hugged Emily. "Let's go outside and talk," said Sarah.

Once they were seated on the grass, far away from anyone else, Emily told them everything.

"Are you happy?" asked Sarah.

"Yeah," Emily said through tears.

"Then, why are you crying?" asked Sarah.

"I thought you'd be mad I didn't tell you right away."

"Good point. You did lie when I asked you about him during the sleepover, but I'll forgive you," Abby said with a laugh.

Emily and Sarah glared at Abby. Emily ripped out blades of grass and continued, "And honestly, I was afraid you'd splatter the juicy details all over the place. That's how I got in trouble with my dad last time. And just as Kevin's telling me not to worry, there's Abby, snapping away."

Both girls stared at Abby, who looked like a kid caught with her hand in the cookie jar.

"Oops. My bad. I'm sorry. I'm like one of those dogs that drools whenever it hears a bell. It's an instinctual reaction," she said while pretending to tap out information on her phone. Emily and Sarah didn't laugh. Abby cleared her throat. "Sorry. Trying but failing to lighten up the mood here. Okay, seriously, I'm sorry about sneaking up on you and Kevin, but, look, I didn't do anything with the picture." She flashed her phone at Emily. "I'll delete it right now. And, I swear I'll keep everything quiet from now on."

"Really? You'd do that for me?" Emily asked quietly.

"Of course," said Abby in her big-sister way. "Like I said at your house, we'll be stealthy social ninjas. No pictures, no detailed posts. I'll write vague stuff, like, 'Out with friends. Having fun' instead of 'Out with ED and KWM. They can't keep their hands off each other long enough to do tequila shots or hit the bong.' How's that?"

"Perfect," Emily said with a chuckle.

"Good, now tell your caveman boyfriend to chill," Abby said. "He knocked my cell out of my hand when you ran off. He's lucky I have a decent case and my phone didn't break."

Abby started to tap out a text message.

"Abigail Rose Carter, what are you doing?" asked Sarah. "Didn't you just promise to lay off the texting?"

"Yes, I did, Sarah Jean Mason, but I'm texting the Neanderthal that we found Emily and everything's cool," said Abby. "That's okay, right? I'm not tweeting about her steamy summer, although I want to. See my eye—it's twitching because I'm restraining myself. Is this a symptom of withdrawal?"

They all laughed again.

"We should head back in," said Sarah. "Lunch is almost over."

"I have to get myself together before I go to class," said Emily. She returned to the last stall in the girls' bathroom and sank to the floor again. She dug out a small makeup bag from her backpack and got to work covering up any signs of crying.

That done, she pushed herself off the ground and inspected herself in the big mirror over the sink before going to class. She was officially dating Kevin. Her friends knew and were actually happy for her. They even promised not to advertise her and Kevin's every move. Her father, then, would stay off her case since there'd be no evidence. *Everything was going to be fine.*

Why, then, didn't she feel light as air, like she could have floated to her next class? She jammed her fingertips against her temples but couldn't squash her headache. She told herself again and again, *Everything's going to be fine*, hoping if she said this often enough, she would soon believe it.

CHAPTER 13

Letter #1

Dear Ms. Diaz,

    I wanted to tell you this after class yesterday, but couldn't. I hope it's okay for me to write to you. In person wouldn't work. This way, I can tell you what I'm really thinking.

    Anyway, yesterday, you asked us about where we dwell—what vehicle we use to understand the world around us. I have vehicles that help me navigate the world, but I don't think I'm figuring anything out. I try, but lately I feel like I'm driving in circles. I ask questions, I think, I write in my journal, but I always end up with more questions. Round and round I go.

    So, yes, I have vehicles to help me navigate the world, but I can't make sense of it.

People think they have me all figured out.

They take one look at me and think they know me,
like it's that easy. But they have no idea. I guess we're
all clueless, even you, Ms. D.

Ms. Diaz photocopied the letter twice—one for her files and
another for Suzanne Gilbert, Elizabeth's guidance counselor.
She put a copy of the letter into Suzanne's mailbox, sealed in
an envelope, with a note: *This was slipped under my door this*
morning. No name. I think it's from Elizabeth Davis. I won't
respond—for now.

CHAPTER 14

"When we have ceased to care"

OCTOBER

Elizabeth plopped onto a plastic chair at a table in the back of the cafeteria. Tommy and Kevin were already there. Before she even opened one of the two bags of chips she bought, she asked, "Do you think teachers really care about their students, or do you think it's an act?"

"I think some care and some don't," said Tommy.

"Like who?" asked Elizabeth.

"Let's go through the list," Kevin suggested and bit his turkey sandwich.

"How about Ms. Diaz?" asked Elizabeth. "This morning she complimented my bangs."

"Hey, nice bangs, by the way," said Kevin.

"I noticed, too," said Tommy.

"Yeah, right. I cut them in July," said Elizabeth.

"See," said Tommy. "I can't win. If I didn't say anything ever, I'd be a jerk for not noticing. If I said your hair looked nice when you first cut it, you would've said, 'What? Didn't it look nice before?'"

"Right, man?" asked Kevin. "Girls are tricky that way." The two nodded and shook hands in a complex way.

"Focus, please," said Elizabeth. "Ms. Diaz does that every day, though. She says good morning and tries to personalize it. Haven't you noticed?"

"What's wrong with that?" asked Tommy.

"Yeah, I think it's kinda nice," said Kevin.

"I just wonder if it's genuine, or if it's something you learn in How-to-Be-a-Teacher one-oh-one."

"Does it really matter?" asked Kevin. "I mean, who cares if she cares? She's a teacher, not your mom."

Tommy kicked Kevin in the shin and shook his head.

"Ow!" Kevin rubbed his leg and eyed Tommy and Elizabeth. He smirked and said, "Maybe you wouldn't care about Ms. D if you had another kind of love in your life."

Tommy kicked Kevin again and Elizabeth threw a chip at his face.

"Jeez, I don't know why I hang out with you two, with all this abuse I take," said Kevin. "You two aren't easy to love, you know that?"

Tommy snickered, but Elizabeth stared at Kevin and then lowered her gaze to the top of the table. Tommy shook his head again at Kevin, trying to get him to cut the comments.

"Sorry, Davis. I was kidding," Kevin said. "I didn't know you were so sensitive. Lighten up, would you?"

"I'm not sensitive, and I don't need to lighten up. You have no idea what you're talking about." Elizabeth raised a hand. "You know what, no. I'm not getting into it with you, and how did this conversation become about me, anyway?"

"Right," said Tommy. He grabbed one of Elizabeth's bags of chips. She let him steal a few chips before she snatched back the bag. "Well, we could survey the teachers. Ask them why they got into teaching, what they like and don't like. It could be an interesting story for the newspaper, don't you think?"

"I guess," said Elizabeth.

"It's too bad you don't write. You could do the article." He grabbed one of her bags of chips again.

"I can write," Elizabeth said defensively. She grabbed back her chips.

"I didn't say you can't write. You don't, though."

"I don't write for the paper. That doesn't mean I don't write."

"Really, so what do you write in your journal?" Tommy asked. Kevin grinned at the exchange.

"Stuff," said Elizabeth.

"So, why not publish any of this stuff in the paper? That is what we do."

"It's not for the paper. It's not meant to be read by anyone else."

"So mysterious," said Kevin.

"You see what I have to deal with?" Tommy asked Kevin.

"What's that supposed to mean?" asked Elizabeth.

"Nothing," said Tommy. The boys glanced at each other and snickered again.

"Girls are complicated," said Kevin. "Like my little *chica*, Emily. *Muy complicada*."

"So, you're paying attention in Spanish class this year? Or are you getting ready to meet her family?" Elizabeth said and laughed. "You never told me how this whole thing with Emily started."

"Well, first, I kissed her at a party in June because Abby asked me to."

"What?"

"How could you not know about the kiss? We went viral. Do you live like the Amish at home or something?"

"I knew about the kiss. Who didn't? I didn't know that Abby told you to do it."

"Neither does Emily. God, she'd kill us both, although, it wasn't like an order or a dare or anything. It was more like a friendly nudge in Em's direction. No big deal."

"Stop saying that. You both say that all the time, even when you know it's a big deal. You drive me crazy."

"I love you, too, Davis. It's not easy, but I do," said Kevin. "Anyway, after that, Emily's dad went ballistic over the whole thing and she dropped me. But, once that died down, we started hanging out again." Kevin paused and looked over at

Emily's lunch table. Elizabeth turned to look, too, but snapped back when Emily glanced in their direction.

"So, then what happened?" asked Elizabeth.

"She wanted to keep it quiet. We argued about that, and one day she went off on me because she said I flirted with Sarah in English class."

"Did you?" asked Tommy.

"No," said Kevin.

"Yes, you did," said Elizabeth. "I remember. On one of the first days of school, you scratched Sarah's back and then winked at Emily. It's like you were flirting with both of them. I meant to slap you for that."

"I needed a pencil. I wasn't flirting."

"Are you kidding?" said Elizabeth. "You could have tapped Sarah on the shoulder or whispered her name to get her attention. Scratching her back was a flirty move."

"Really? I should run some of this stuff by you from now on, Davis. I mean, you are a girl."

"Excellent observation skills, Kev."

"Thanks," he said. "I mean, I feel weird asking my dads about advice on women."

"They know way more about having a successful relationship than you do," said Elizabeth.

"True. Anyway, I convinced Emily I wasn't flirting, promised her everything would be fine, and we've been great since then." Kevin smiled as he dragged a french fry through a blob of ketchup.

"Do you really like her?" asked Elizabeth.

"Yeah."

"Was it her first time?"

Kevin nodded.

Elizabeth looked over at Emily. She sat at the end of a table filled with popular sophomore girls. A paper napkin lay unfolded on her lap, as if she were in a restaurant. She bit off small pieces of her sandwich and chewed with her mouth closed. She listened attentively to her friends but didn't talk much.

Elizabeth turned back when Emily caught her staring again. She remembered finding Emily on the bathroom floor a month ago. *If things were so great, why was she a sobbing mess?*

"Here's what I think: Everyone knows you're a flirt, but if that little scratch bothered her so much, then don't flirt with anyone in the slightest, especially not her best friends. And if you ever break up, you can never date Sarah or Abby. Cross them off your list."

"Yeah?"

"Yeah. Trust me on this. I'm a girl, remember?"

"This is true," said Kevin, "but you don't have girlfriends. I mean, you hang out with guys, so are you sure? Like if we made out and then Tommy wanted to date you, I really wouldn't care. I'm not saying I want to kiss you, although I wouldn't turn you away either, and I'm not saying Tommy wants to date you. I'm just saying guys are different and you hang out with guys, not girls."

Elizabeth sat quiet while Tommy rubbed his temples.

"Three things," Elizabeth said to Kevin. "One, shut up. Two, don't make her any more promises. Three, take my advice."

"Okay, then . . . Sarah and Abby are off the list forever, no big deal."

Elizabeth leaned over and punched Kevin in the arm.

"Damn, Davis," he said as he rubbed the spot.

"I'm going to hit you every time you say that," she said. "You, too." She pointed at Tommy, who held up his hands in surrender.

"Before we get off the topic of girls, I must say that Abby is all about you, Tommy Boy." Kevin playfully punched Tommy on the arm.

"Hey, man, cut it out," Tommy said. He glared at Kevin and glanced at Elizabeth. She noticed but didn't say anything.

When the bell rang, the boys turned to face the doors that led to the main hallway. Elizabeth turned in the other direction toward a door leading outside.

"Hey, where are you going?" asked Tommy.

"I need a break," she said.

"You're going to get caught," Tommy yelled at her as she walked away from him. "Teachers take attendance every period. They'll know you're missing."

"I know," she yelled back over her shoulder. "And I don't care."

CHAPTER 15

"Pain has but one Acquaintance"

In the nearby wooded area, Elizabeth climbed on a large downed tree. She sat on top of it, carefully placed one leg on each side of the trunk, and leaned back with her hands linked behind her head. She closed her eyes and breathed deeply. The warm autumn sun kissed her face; the chilled wind gently followed with a light caress. This beat P.E. class any day. The detention would be worth it.

After resting for a while, Elizabeth opened her eyes. White clouds streaked a soothing light-blue sky. The trees' tallest branches stretched and waved in the mid-October wind. Lush evergreens mingled with their colorful, shedding neighbors. Elizabeth looked a little lower at a branch perfect for climbing.

She sprang to her feet and scanned the tree for nooks to

help her climb. She placed a foot here and grabbed a branch there; she hoisted herself and repeated the movements to reach the tempting branch. She straddled the branch, lay flat on her belly, and shimmied out as far as she could go. She turned her face against the branch, hugging it tight and laughing with pleasure.

Elizabeth remembered climbing trees with her dad. When she was little, he'd place her on a branch and hold her by the waist. Later, he'd guide her from the ground as she climbed, a little higher each year. If she got scared, he calmed her by promising: "I'm right here. I won't let you get hurt."

The wind blew over Elizabeth again, making her wobble. If the branch snapped, she'd get hurt. No serious damage, but enough to matter.

The fastest and easiest way down was to hang from the branch and then let go, being sure to bend at the knees when she hit the ground to protect her legs. This was another thing Dad taught her: "If you're going to take risks, you have to know how to protect yourself." She unlocked her legs, gripped the branch, and turned to dangle.

She wondered: If a student fell in the woods, and no one was there to hear her, would she make a sound?

She laughed at herself.

And then her hands slipped.

She didn't have time to prepare her landing. She fell on her side, her leg bent under her weight. Her face scrunched in pain—eyes shut tight, teeth clenched. She rolled on her back and held her knee. Her mouth opened, but the sharp, immediate pain stole her breath and deadened her scream. When she was able to, she arched her back and released a loud, guttural groan.

She stayed down, looking at the branch that now mocked her. Once the pain dulled a bit, she pushed herself into a sitting position. She breathed deeply for a few minutes before she tried to straighten her leg, knowing this would bring another wave of pain. She moved slowly like this, extending her leg, shifting her weight, breathing through the pain, until she was able to stand.

Now, she knew: He wouldn't be there. She *would* get hurt. And, yeah, if a student fell in the woods, and no one was there, she'd make a sound, a horrible one.

But no one would hear her.

Good to know.

Elizabeth figured she'd miss her science and Spanish classes if the school nurse let her rest after checking out the damage, but she was going up against Mrs. Ryan, a graduate of the Nurse Ratched Training School. She wasn't stupid and had a tough-as-nails attitude with frequent fliers, like Elizabeth, who overused the go-to-the-nurse-to-get-out-of-class plan. Mrs. Ryan poked Elizabeth's knee with the delicacy of a jackhammer and concluded that nothing appeared broken or dislocated. She handed Elizabeth an ice pack and a pass and sent her hobbling back to class.

Halfway through Biology, the phone rang. Elizabeth was wanted in Guidance. She limped into Ms. Gilbert's office to discuss why she skipped gym. The assistant principal, who

usually handled discipline, let Ms. Gilbert relay the consequence since everyone considered Elizabeth a "sensitive case."

Today, though, Ms. Gilbert wasn't gushing with compas-
sion. That was last year's approach when Elizabeth's wounds
were fresh. Ms. Gilbert sat behind her desk, not in one of
the nearby comfy chairs. She removed the basket of stress-
reliever knickknacks from reach so that she had Elizabeth's
full attention.

"Your consequence is to make up the P.E. class by walking
the track after school for forty-five minutes," Ms. Gilbert
said with little sympathy in her voice.

"But, I sprained my knee when I fell from the tree," Elizabeth protested. She sat straight up. She wanted to prop her
leg on Ms. Gilbert's desk, but instead crossed her legs and
placed the ice pack on the side of her knee. "Making me walk
for forty-five minutes is cruel and unusual punishment, and
I'm pretty sure we have laws against that."

"Well, the nurse says your injury isn't serious, so you should
be fine," Ms. Gilbert responded. "Unless you have a doctor's
note or your mom excuses you for some reason, you will make
up the class."

"I'm not calling my mom," Elizabeth said indignantly.

"Fine, then you'll make up the class." Ms. Gilbert's arms
were crossed; her elbows rested on the desk. "Anyway, I
think that's more fitting than having detention. You should
make up any class you skip because the point is we want you
in class and nowhere else. Every teacher has something valu-
able to teach you. That's why they're here. When you miss a

class, you miss something important and you send the message that you don't care."

"I don't care? Seriously? I hurt my knee, and you want me to walk for forty-five minutes, and I am the one who shows a lack of caring?" She was animated as she spoke, moving her hands and pointing at herself and Ms. Gilbert to emphasize her point.

Ms. Gilbert sat quiet for a moment and then said, "Elizabeth, you should know by now that I am deeply concerned about your well-being."

Elizabeth sighed and lowered her gaze. She uncrossed her legs and slouched in her seat a bit. She stretched out her leg, trying but failing to ease her discomfort.

"This is not about me right now. This is about you, and yes, when you skip class, you send the message that you don't care."

"That I don't care about what?"

"About anything. About the class, the teacher, what they have to offer you, your education, yourself."

"All of that because I skipped gym?" Elizabeth asked sarcastically. Tears welled up. She swallowed hard, trying to stop them.

"This isn't only about P.E. class," Ms. Gilbert said, pulling back a little, uncrossing her arms. "It's a new school year. I don't want last year's routines to be repeated. I want you to focus on this year and not dwell in the past. The reality is, Elizabeth, you can't go back and change what happened."

Ms. Gilbert paused again. Elizabeth looked down at a small

hole in her jeans, new from the fall. She pulled at it with her fingers. She often did that, made small things bigger instead of leaving them alone.

"What you can change is yourself, how you do things, how you feel, how you see and respond to the world. But you have to *want* things to change. And you have to care *more* than the people around you."

"I care," Elizabeth said softly, still pulling at the hole in her jeans.

"Look at me," demanded Ms. Gilbert. Elizabeth straightened up a bit and raised her eyes. Ms. Gilbert stared right at her. "Then, prove it."

Elizabeth lowered her gaze again and began to cry. Ms. Gilbert let her tears fall for a minute and then handed her a box of tissues. Elizabeth plucked one and wiped her face. Most of her black eyeliner streaked off after several swift strokes. Ms. Gilbert wrote Elizabeth a pass to class and handed it to her. "You can start by going to every class, every day."

Elizabeth snatched the pass and left without another word.

After school, Elizabeth entered the girls' gym locker room to get ready for her makeup class. She had a new ice pack and an Ace bandage thanks to Nurse Ryan, and she had duct tape thanks to her tech-ed teacher. Sitting on a bench, she leaned over, wrapped the flexible ice pack around her knee and secured it as best she could with the Ace bandage. Then, she unrolled a long piece of duct tape, ripped it with her teeth, and wrapped it around her knee.

Nearby, Emily watched Elizabeth. She noiselessly closed her locker after changing for cross-country practice.

"Are you okay?" she asked in almost a whisper.

"I'm fantastic, can't you tell?" Elizabeth responded but didn't look at Emily.

"Sorry. Is there anything I can do?"

"Yeah, leave me alone." Elizabeth turned and glared at Emily. Her tone and words were harsh, but her eyes revealed something else. Emily stared back, a bit stunned. She opened her mouth to say something, but turned and jogged out of the locker room. Elizabeth pushed herself off the bench and followed Emily's steps, limping out of the locker room and to the track.

Elizabeth cut to the inside lane and observed the packs of runners. Some talked and laughed while they ran. Others were serious, concentrating on their breathing and pacing. On the other side of the track, she spotted Abby, who looked like she was skipping through a meadow, turning at times as she talked to Sarah, like she was telling a story and choreographing it at the same time. Emily jogged behind this running-dancing-laughing twosome, struggling to catch up.

Elizabeth felt bad about snapping at Emily, but her own misery overruled any stitch of sympathy she had for anyone else. Walking casually was all Elizabeth could manage. Whenever she tried to pick up her pace, pain shot through her knee. She winced and tears stung her eyes.

As Elizabeth rounded a corner, she looked beyond the track to the nearby parking lot. Ms. Diaz stood next to her car. She raised a hand just above her eyes, like a visor, and watched the activity on the track. After a few paces, Elizabeth realized that Ms. Diaz was looking directly at her.

Maybe she does care. For a second, she asked herself the same question Kevin asked at lunch, *"Who cares if she cares?"* She hadn't shared it at lunch, but she had a reason. She needed Ms. Diaz to care because somebody had to. And it had to be someone who wasn't required to because they were family or receiving a paycheck to be "concerned about her well-being."

Elizabeth used the collar of her T-shirt to wipe away her tears. If Ms. Diaz wasn't tired of her yet, then maybe Elizabeth could muster the energy to care. Ms. Diaz lifted the hand she used to shield her eyes to give Elizabeth a wave. Elizabeth didn't respond. With her eyes fixed a few inches in front of her feet, she continued to hobble around the track.

CHAPTER 16

"I can't tell you –
but you feel it –"

"Here you are," said Sarah as she slipped into a chair across from Emily in the school library. Abby dropped her heavy backpack to the floor near the table and sat next to Sarah. She faced Emily, but turned her body sideways and crossed her legs.

"Hey," Emily said and smiled.

"We decided to hunt you down when you didn't show at lunch. Are you okay?" asked Sarah, who leaned into the table to get as close to Emily as possible.

"I'm fine," said Emily.

"No, you're not," said Abby. Emily tensed and sat up straighter. "You've got to be so much more than fine when you're in love with Kevin Wen-Massey. If you say you're just fine, I'll be so disappointed."

The girls laughed loud enough to earn a stern stare and a "Shush!" from the librarian.

"Is that why you haven't been hanging out with us much? Has Kevin been taking up all of your time?" Sarah asked and raised an eyebrow.

"Enough with the eyebrows," Emily said and chuckled. "What do you mean? I've been hanging out with you guys."

"In school, yeah, sort of, but out of school, you've been totally M.I.A.," said Abby. "The last six weekends, you've missed two trips to the mall, two group hangouts at Angelo's Pizza, one party, and a movie. I don't remember what it was about, but Ryan Gosling was in it, so it was awesome."

The girls laughed.

"Not that we're keeping track or anything," Sarah said and glared at Abby.

"I'm just saying if you're going to blow us off, I hope it's worth it."

"Sounds like you've been out more than me," said Emily. "I mean, yeah, I've been hanging out with Kevin, but I've been busy with other things, too." Emily pointed to the opened books in front of her.

"Busy with something other than Kevin? What could possibly be more interesting or fun?" Abby swiveled her legs under the table and faced Emily to be fully into the conversation.

"You know, schoolwork and things at home. And, when I'm done with all of that, I'm tired."

"Tired? You're sixteen, not sixty, Em," said Abby. "Listen, down a couple of Red Bulls this week because Lucas is having a party on Saturday and we're going. And by 'we,' I mean the three of us. Kevin can meet us there if he wants, okay?"

Going to a party was the last thing Emily wanted to do, but she said, "Okay."

The house was packed when they arrived. Sarah and Abby moved easily through the crowd, saying hi to people. Sarah was in front of Emily, holding her hand as they walked. Emily focused on Sarah's hand wrapped around hers, remembering how they used to clasp hands as they sat side by side on the playground swings. They'd see how high they could go without getting out of sync and disconnected.

In the kitchen, Abby made her way to a senior named Sergio who was pouring drinks. She tugged on the front of his shirt to get him to bend down. He smiled at whatever she said, and she pecked him on the cheek when he handed her the first of three cups of beer. Abby kept one and passed the others to Sarah and Emily. They "clinked" their plastic cups and Sarah and Abby drank. Emily held her cup low and scanned the room.

"Abby, move in," Sarah said. "We'll shield you," she said to Emily. Once concealed, Emily gulped her drink.

"There you go," said Abby. She grabbed Emily by the shoulders and shook her gently. "Loosen up and have fun. No worries, okay? The social ninja warriors have your back."

Abby and Emily smiled and then Abby turned her attention back to Sergio.

"Come on, let's walk around," said Sarah.

Sarah guided Emily through the house and outside. When Sarah stopped to talk to some people, Emily kept walking. She went back inside and weaved through the crowd several times looking for Kevin, but he hadn't arrived yet. When her beer was gone, she returned to the kitchen for another. Abby was kissing Sergio, so someone else managed the beer-pouring duties. Emily slyly sipped her drink when no one was looking and smiled politely when they were. Her stomach twisted in knots. She wanted to go home but didn't say anything.

Instead, Emily went upstairs and discovered an office. She closed the door behind her almost all the way, but left it open just enough to allow in a sliver of light from the hallway. Books lined one wall, from ceiling to floor. She found an old, hardcover copy of Thoreau's *Walden* and sat near the door. Legs stretched out and ankles crossed, Emily relaxed and read as best she could with the dim light. She quickly got lost in the pages.

After a while, the door opened. Before Emily could move, someone tripped over her legs. The girl clutched a large cup in one hand that she didn't want to spill, so she instinctively twisted and landed with a thud.

"Ugh! Not again!" Elizabeth rolled on her back. She groaned and pounded her fist into the hardwood floor, once for each word: "Son of a bitch!"

Emily covered her mouth with her hand, half-worried about Elizabeth and half laughing at the girl's reaction.

Elizabeth stared at the ceiling for a few moments before turning to see who had caused her fall.

"Delgado, what are you doing here?"

"Reading."

"Reading. Of course. That makes total sense." Elizabeth sat up and moved opposite Emily, her back against the wall, her knees hugged to her chest. She alternately rubbed her injured leg and rolled the wrist that saved her face from hitting the floor.

Emily stood and pushed the door back in place. "What are *you* doing here?" she asked after returning to her spot on the floor. "You hardly ever come to parties."

"Right. I should have kept that up, too," said Elizabeth. "First, I thought it was a stupid Halloween costume party, and then I thought this was the bathroom. Now, I'm hurt. I should have stayed home as usual, but no, I let Tommy drag me here. He's going to pay for this."

Emily took a good look at Elizabeth. Her hair was in pigtails. She wore ripped jean shorts, fishnet stockings, a black-and-red dog collar, and black knee-length leather boots with rows of metal buckles.

"Don't you always dress kind of like that?"

"I had on a white lab coat and NCIS badge. I left it in the car when I saw no one else was dressed. I brought this, though, figuring I'd need to drink to get through the night." Elizabeth reached for the large cup she managed to save during the fall. It read "Caf-Pow." She sucked hard on the straw.

"You look like her," Emily said with a smile.

"Yeah, well, I figured it would be easy enough. I own the same freakish clothes."

"I think she's beautiful," said Emily.

Elizabeth squinted her eyes at Emily but didn't say anything. After a few quiet moments, Elizabeth asked, "Why are you in here reading?"

"I didn't want to come to the party, either."

"Why not? Kevin's here."

"Did he come with you?" Emily asked.

Elizabeth nodded.

Just then, Emily's phone buzzed, a text from Kevin, asking where she was. She responded that she was in the bathroom and would find him later.

"I know it's none of my business, but why did you wait so long to tell your friends? I mean, Abby's shoving her tongue down Sergio's throat in the middle of the kitchen. Did you really think they'd care?"

Emily thought for a moment. *Why* had *she kept it a secret?*

"At first, I thought they'd be mad because I didn't tell them right when it happened. And then, I blasted Kevin for flirting with Sarah, but I guess I overreacted. And, I'm *always* worried about slipping up because of my dad."

"You're a liar," said Elizabeth.

Emily flinched. "What?"

"I don't mean you're lying about what you told me. I'm sure all of that is true, but you're still lying to them."

Emily looked confused, but Elizabeth went on, "Lying's the worst. People freak out—I mean, like screaming, punching, crying kind of freak out—when they're lied to. Like when someone asks, 'Are you okay?' and she says, 'I'm fine.' And the person asks, 'Are you sure?' and she says, 'Yes, leave me alone.' Lies. All lies."

"You're right. I lied to you that day in the bathroom," said Emily. "But you lied to me in the locker room."

"Maybe, but let me finish my story. Now, if this girl told the truth, she'd say, 'I'm thinking about dropping out of high school and joining the circus because I'm pretty sure shoveling elephant shit all day would be better than sticking around here.' But, instead, she lies to make it easy on people. And you know what? It doesn't matter because they know she's lying and she still gets labeled the 'troubled child' who needs fixing and everyone becomes focused on her instead of the lie that set her off in the first place."

With wide eyes, Emily asked, "Are you okay?"

"I'm fine." Elizabeth smiled and sucked hard on her straw.

"You're lying," Emily said with a grin.

"Maybe, but this isn't about me. It's about you. Tell them. Get it over with, Delgado."

Emily shook her head and hugged the book to her chest. "Tell them what?"

Elizabeth stared at Emily. They were quiet, listening to voices in the hallway and the music pounding below them, so loud the floorboards vibrated.

Elizabeth sprang forward from her sitting position and crawled the few feet that separated her from Emily. She kneeled and sat back on her heels.

"Look at me," she whispered. Emily pushed her back into the wall and locked gazes with Elizabeth.

Elizabeth scanned Emily's face and then framed the girl's eyes with her fingers.

"Ah, there it is," said Elizabeth.

"What?"

"Hold still." Elizabeth pressed down her index finger, closed her eyes, and said, "Click."

"What are you doing?" asked Emily.

"I'm taking a mental picture of you." Elizabeth leaned in closer. Emily inhaled sharply.

"I *see* you, Emily Delgado," she whispered. "Your problem isn't really about your friends or Kevin or your dad. You try to hide it, but I know." Elizabeth patted Emily's leg. "Trust me, I know."

"You're drunk."

"Maybe, but you know what I mean." Elizabeth popped up to her feet, crossed the room to her previous spot, and grabbed her cup. She sucked hard on the straw and shook the empty cup. "And now I really do need to find the bathroom." She walked toward the door and half turned back to Emily.

"I know we're not friends or anything, but if you want to hang with Kevin at lunch, you can sit with us. I'll warn you, though. I've been told I'm hard to love. Being close to me is kind of like cuddling up with a rattlesnake. You take your chances."

Before Emily could respond, Elizabeth was gone.

Emily stayed in the room until her eyes couldn't take any more reading in the near-dark. When she found Abby and Sarah, they smiled and continued to talk with the people around them. They didn't ask her where she had been. When Kevin spotted her, he swept her up in a bear hug and gave her a kiss. Emily gulped her beer in dark corners and clung to Kevin for the rest of the night, burying her face in his chest whenever people posed for pictures.

Finally, Abby and Sarah wanted to leave. As they waited outside for Abby's older brother to pick them up, they popped gum into their mouths to hide the smell of alcohol. Emily stared at the concrete, trying to stop her world from spinning.

"Did you have fun?" Abby asked.

"Yeah," she lied.

During the ride home and while she lay in bed, Emily mentally replayed the conversation she had with Elizabeth in the dark room until she fell asleep or passed out—she wasn't sure which.

The next morning, Emily woke up early to go to church with her family. A sharp pain ran through her head. The smells of breakfast turned her stomach, so she passed.

Sitting in the pew, Emily couldn't concentrate. Parts of her felt restless, but her limbs and head were heavy. The priest's words were like needles stabbing through her nausea. He preached about Jacob wrestling with God through the night. About struggles and unshaken faith and not giving up even though he was injured.

Emily looked at Mamá and Pop and thought about her friends and Kevin. Like Jacob, they all had struggles, but none of them had faced a major tragedy. She watched the news. Compared to others, her life and her problems were pretty ordinary. So why did it all *feel* like she was in an epic battle? Why did every snarky remark become a festering wound? Why did she always feel like she was pinned to the mat and crushed under their weight? Why wasn't she as strong as Jacob?

After the sermon, Emily concentrated on her footing while walking down the aisle for Holy Communion. The host stuck to her tongue, which made her mouth water. When she swallowed a sip of wine, her stomach lurched. She turned down a side aisle, pushed open a door to the outside, and vomited on the sidewalk.

CHAPTER 17

"Death is the supple Suitor"

NOVEMBER

Elizabeth sat in Tommy's kitchen, where rows of small white skulls covered the table. She scanned the sugar candies and selected one to decorate.

"That's the one, huh?" Tommy asked as he joined her. "How do you choose when they all look the same?"

"One speaks to me each year," she said seriously.

"O-kay," said Tommy.

"She understands death," said Mrs. Bowles, as she delivered to the table plastic pastry bags packed with colorful icing.

"Actually, I've seen services at the cemetery, but I haven't attended a funeral yet." Elizabeth filled the hollows of her skull's eyes with yellow icing and outlined them with purple.

"Doesn't matter," said Mrs. Bowles. "You still understand

death. I could tell from the first time you helped us to distribute marigolds on *El Día de los Muertos*. You understand the need to respect death as we do life, which is why we remember and honor those who have passed. A poem often recited during the holiday is: 'What is death? It is the glass of life broken into a thousand pieces, where the soul disperses like perfume from a flask, into the silence of the eternal night.'"

"That one always brings a tear to my eye, hon," said Mr. Bowles as he entered the kitchen. He crossed the room, ignored his wife's hand on her hip, and both kissed her cheek and patted her backside at the same time.

"Seriously, you two? Jeez, just ignore them," Tommy said to Elizabeth.

"I think they're cute," she said.

"Really? So if I tried that with you . . ."

"I'd chop your hand off," she finished.

Mr. Bowles laughed, while Mrs. Bowles winked at Elizabeth. Tommy was a cool blend of his parents. He got his height from Dad and his eyes from Mom. His brown, shaggy hair was the result of his dad's straight, light-brown hair mixed with his mom's almost black ringlets.

"Anyway, I was talking to Elizabeth, not you, Connor," said Mrs. Bowles.

"*Lo siento, querida*," he said and pecked her again. "Hey, Elizabeth, did I ever tell you the two Spanish phrases I learned before asking Elena to marry me? '*Sí, querida*' and '*Lo siento, querida*.'"

"You're a smart man, Mr. Bowles," Elizabeth said and grinned at Mrs. Bowles. Elizabeth created a red heart on her skull's forehead. Swirls of blue and dots of orange covered its cheeks and the top of its head, while its teeth were outlined in black, tiny lines separating each tooth.

Mr. Bowles sat across from Elizabeth, chose two skulls, and did his best to decorate one in green and orange and another in red and blue to honor his dead Irish and British ancestors.

"Anyway, souls are immortal," continued Mrs. Bowles. "Like the living, they don't want to be ignored. Like us, too, they enjoy a good party, which is why we drink and eat and make candies and tell funny stories."

"Do you remember when Great-Granddad saw the smoke from the grill and thought the porch was on fire, so he busted through the screen door?" said Mr. Bowles. "He yelled, 'Bloody hell, Connor, who puts a grill so close to the house?' like it was my fault and it was perfectly reasonable for him to think the porch was in flames."

Everyone laughed hard.

"Or the time Abuela was cleaning out the big square garbage can and she bent over to scrub down low and she fell inside," said Tommy.

"She's lucky she didn't break anything and, *Dios mío*, did she swear like a sailor that day," Mrs. Bowles said and wiped her eyes. She nodded. "It's good to laugh *and* cry. Too much crying without laughing is bad for the soul."

Mrs. Bowles wiped her eyes once more and said, "What a

sight, with her legs sticking out of the can." She chuckled and added, *"¿Quiere café?"*

"Sí, querida," said Mr. Bowles.

"I was talking to Elizabeth," she said and smiled.

"Sí, gracias," said Elizabeth as she reached for a new skull to beautify.

The next day, Tommy and Elizabeth sat beneath the weeping willow in the cemetery after embellishing the tombstones with marigolds and bedazzled candy skulls. Elizabeth rested the first skull she selected the day before next to Sophia Holland's headstone.

Mrs. Bowles offered Tommy and Elizabeth a blanket and bagged lunches before she left.

"Your mom's the best," said Elizabeth as she removed a sandwich from the bag. She held up a napkin and plastic utensils. "She thinks of everything."

"Yeah," said Tommy. "She's a keeper."

Elizabeth retrieved her marble design–covered journal from her bag. While she ate, she alternately glanced over the cemetery and jotted down notes.

Tommy inched toward her and extended his neck to view the page.

"If you get any closer, I'll stab you in the eye with my pencil," she said.

"The point of the holiday is to honor death, not encourage it," said Tommy.

Elizabeth giggled and continued her work in her note-book.

"So, whatcha got in there?" Tommy asked and craned his neck again.

"Random thoughts, poems, sketches, et cetera."

"Can I . . . ?"

"No," she said, cutting him off.

Tommy sighed. "You know, I read somewhere that to remain alive in the physical world after death, a person should procreate or publish."

"What are you suggesting, Tomás?" Elizabeth asked with a raised eyebrow.

"Well, we're too young to have babies. I mean, we're not technically, but I'd rather wait, so the only real option right now is to publish."

"Well, then, mission accomplished," said Elizabeth. "You've had lots of articles published in the school news-paper. I'll call you the Immortal Mr. Bowles from now on."

"I like the way that sounds," he said and rubbed his clean-shaven chin.

"According to your mom, the soul is immortal, so we don't have to do anything to live forever. No books or babies required."

"Right, but if you want to be remembered in the physical world, you should leave something physical behind," said Tommy. "Think about it, a child is likely to have children, and so on and so on, and a published work lives forever. We wouldn't still be talking about Shakespeare or Dickinson if they didn't create something that was eventually shared with the world."

"True, so, I ask again, what are you suggesting, Tomás?"

"You should publish something in the newspaper."

"My photos are published all the time. That's art, so consider me immortalized."

"Yeah, but you could do more, like write articles or publish something from your secret journal there."

Elizabeth remained quiet for a minute. She closed her notebook and clutched it to her chest. "Taking pictures for the newspaper is different. Those aren't personal. What I write in here is. And I can't go around stabbing everyone who hates it," she said, jabbing her pencil up and down.

"True, but will you think about it?"

"Sure," she said. "I'll consider it, on one condition."

"What's that?"

"I get to eat your Dead Bread," she said with a smile.

"I don't have any *Pan de Muerto*."

"Liar! Your mom put a piece in my bag, so you must have one, too."

"Clearly, she likes you more," said Tommy as he opened his paper sack wide to show her the absence of sweets.

"Like I said, your mom's the best." Elizabeth ripped her piece of bread in half and offered it to Tommy.

"Thanks," he said and took a bite.

After eating, Elizabeth lay on her side, her bag beneath her head like a pillow. She patted the space beside her.

"Nap time?" Tommy asked with a smile.

"Yeah. I couldn't sleep last night."

"Shocker," he said and lay down next to her.

"I know, right?" She forced a smile and closed her eyes. "Poke me in the side if I snore, okay?"

"If you're sleeping so soundly that you're snoring, I definitely will not poke you." He gently removed a small leaf from her hair. "You deserve to rest in peace."

Elizabeth glared at him.

"I mean it, not in a creepy way," he said with a smile and closed his eyes. "Besides, I'm going to join you, so I won't know if you're snoring. We'll both R.I.P., me and double-E.D."

"Please don't ever publish your own poetry," she said with a laugh.

After a while, Tommy fell asleep. Elizabeth gazed at him through partially opened lids and inhaled and exhaled when he did, in the same slow, steady rhythm. Eventually, she dozed off, but her slumber didn't last long. She was startled awake when a newly felled leaf landed on her cheek.

CHAPTER 18

My Letter to the World

Do you know the side effects of sleep deprivation, Ms. Diaz?

Fatigue (duh, right?), memory problems, feeling weak, irritable, depressed.

I didn't need to look this up anywhere, although I did google it to see if my pessimism was a real medical condition or simply my personality. Seriously, though, I couldn't sleep. Not for a long time. And when I did doze off, I had nightmares.

I had one over and over, of a plane crashing into the ocean. Sometimes I'd wake up as soon as the plane hit the water and broke into pieces. Other times, I'd find myself underwater, able to see and breathe. I was calm, looking up at the light above the water's surface.

A few times, I tried to swim to the top. I kicked and pushed with my arms, but about halfway up, I couldn't breathe underwater anymore. Salt water filled my nose and mouth. I fought to get to the top, but never made it. The illuminated surface was just out of reach.

I knew then something deep down inside me was broken. It was the tiniest of cracks, like a pebble hitting a windshield on the highway—plink. No big deal, right? Wait a while. The crack will deepen and spread and permanently damage the once-strong glass.

So, WWEDW? What Would Emily Dickinson Write?

Maybe this: "I felt a Funeral, in my Brain . . . And then a Plank in Reason, broke, / And I dropped down, and down –"

Yeah, that. Exactly that.

Did Emily Dickinson pull away from the world because it was easier and safer to hide than face it all? Or did something inside of her crack? Was something really wrong with her, the way something was really wrong with me? No one seems to know for sure about her. No one really knew about me.

I mean, something was obviously off, but I didn't want to get into it. It was none of their business.

I had to do something, though, because I needed to sleep. So I did what Emily Dickinson wouldn't do. I went to Mom. Yeah, I know, bad move. I should've stuck with her idea that "I never had a mother" because she's not the person I turn to with problems. I guess that shows how desperate I was. Or hopeful, maybe, that she would be like other moms for once. That she'd listen and care.

I told her about the dreams and was ready to tell her more, but she stopped me. She walked into the bathroom, opened the medicine cabinet, grabbed a bottle of pills, and popped off the cap. I opened my hand and she tapped one into my palm. "Take half," she said. "They're strong."

Thanks, Mom, for making it crystal clear that we can never have a conversation about anything that matters because you're too wrapped up in your own problems to unravel mine. Got it.

The next morning, I wanted to thank her for real, though. I didn't remember anything from the night before. No dreams. No nightmares. Nothing. At first, this freaked me out, but then I was relieved. I mean, think about it. My plank in reason broke and I was dropping down and down. Eventually, I'd hit the ground and shatter. Hanging out in Limbo Land for a while seemed like a good alternative. I knew it was a temporary fix, but it was better than falling from planes or planks or anything else.

CHAPTER 19

"I was the slightest
in the House –"

"Good morning, everyone," Ms. Diaz said as she closed her classroom door. "Today, you're going to work in pairs, so the first thing I want to do is . . ."

"Can we pick our partner?" asked Kevin.

"No. The first thing I want to do is move the desks into pairs facing each other."

Ms. Diaz directed the students as they moved the desks into place. She then pointed—"You and you, here; you and you, there"—and handed each pair a folder. Emily raised her eyebrows when she was paired with Elizabeth, but she didn't say anything.

"Are you serious?" asked Elizabeth. "I sit next to her every day. Can't I work with someone else?"

"I put a lot of thought into this, Elizabeth. Emily is a good writer . . ."

"And I'm not?"

Some students giggled. Others watched intently.

"I didn't say that. Let me finish, please. Emily is an exceptional writer. You are a talented artist. Considering today's assignment, I think you'll be great partners."

Emily, who was dressed in gray cargo pants and a simple white, long-sleeved shirt, immediately sat down, circled a piece of hair over her ear, and opened the folder to read every word of the directions.

Elizabeth sauntered to her seat from across the room, where she had been talking with Tommy and Kevin. She sat opposite Emily but didn't say anything. Instead, she retrieved a copy of *Jane Eyre* from her bag, opened it to a folded-over page, and read.

Once everyone was seated, Ms. Diaz said, "Inside the folder, you'll find a poem and some background information. Each pair has a different poem. You'll also find a handout with directions. Take that out and let's go over it."

Since Emily had already studied the directions, she handed them to Elizabeth. She put her book down, picked the paper up, and scanned it.

Once everyone had the handout in front of them, Ms. Diaz continued. "Working with your partner, you'll read the poem and analyze it in writing and visually. You'll hand in a paper, no more than three pages, that analyzes the overall meaning of the poem, highlighting the literary devices."

"What's a literary device?" asked Kevin.

"In your folder, I have included a list of literary devices and their definitions."

"You're my favorite teacher, Ms. D. Have I told you that?" asked Kevin.

"Yeah, yeah," she said, smiling and waving a dismissive hand at him. "Along with the paper, you'll also hand in a visual representation of the poem."

"What if you can't draw?" asked Tommy. "Because I am a stick-figure kind of guy."

"If you read the directions with me," she said pointedly, "then you'll see that you don't have to draw. You may draw, but you may also use clip art or other images from the computer. You may even do an old-fashioned collage with words and images from newspapers and magazines."

"Can we act it out?" asked Kevin. "Or do an interpretive dance?" He waved his arms, which made him look like he was flying rather than dancing. Sarah giggled loudly from her nearby seat, and Abby, who sat close to her, playfully slapped her arm and shushed her. Emily noticed the exchange between the girls, but didn't respond or try to get their attention.

Kevin winked at Emily. She smiled and quickly looked down at the top of her desk.

"No," Ms. Diaz said while smiling.

"Aw, man. I don't know if you're my favorite teacher anymore."

"I'm heartbroken," she joked.

She waited a few moments to let her students consider the assignment.

"I'll walk around and answer any questions. Since today's Friday, let's have it due Wednesday. If you want extra credit, you can present your work to the class before handing it in. I'll give you the rest of the class time to get started."

Elizabeth watched Emily as she took out her notebook and a pencil, and opened the folder she received from Ms. Diaz. Neither said anything. Emily read silently. Elizabeth continued to watch her. She scanned the room and realized they were the only pair not talking to each other.

"What are you reading? Is that the poem?" asked Elizabeth.

Emily glanced up at Elizabeth and looked back down at the paper.

"No. This is some background information."

Elizabeth waited for more, but Emily didn't say anything.

"And . . ." Elizabeth led her. "What does it say?"

"You want me to read it out loud?"

"Well, yeah."

"Oh, sorry." Emily circled her hair around her ear again, cleared her throat, and read:

" 'As a woman in Puritanical New England, Dickinson had few options socially or professionally. She was expected to marry and have children. She was not expected to work outside the home. Even her work as a writer was limited. Women at the time published under men's names. Most wrote prose, not poetry, and those who did write avoided expressing what would be considered controversial ideas.' "

She paused for a moment and looked at Elizabeth. Her elbow was on the desk and her head was tilted, resting in her hand. Elizabeth made a circular motion with her other hand and said, "Go on."

" 'Society's restricted expectations for women were reinforced at home. While Emily's father wanted and allowed his daughters to be educated, they weren't expected to accomplish much after their schooling. Emily Dickinson was well aware of the different standards for men and women. Her frustrations and criticisms were expressed in her poetry.' "

Emily looked up at Elizabeth when she finished but said nothing.

"Now what?" asked Elizabeth. "Where's the poem?"

"Here it is. Do you want me to read that, too?"

"I'll read it. I don't want you to do all the work and then accuse me of being a slacker."

Emily didn't respond. She wasn't sure if Elizabeth was joking. Elizabeth didn't clarify it for her. She leaned over, grabbed the folder with the poem, and read it aloud:

Poem #486
I was the slightest in the House –
I took the smallest Room –
At night, my little Lamp, and Book –
And one Geranium –

So stationed I could catch the Mint
That never ceased to fall –
And just my Basket –
Let me think – I'm sure
That this was all –

I never spoke – unless addressed –
And then, 'twas brief and low –
I could not bear to live – aloud –
The Racket shamed me so –

And if it had not been so far –
And any one I knew
Were going – I had often thought
How noteless – I could die –

"So, how do you want to do this?" asked Elizabeth.

"I don't know," said Emily.

Elizabeth squinted her eyes at Emily. What was her deal? Was she trying to be difficult? Or was she not sure what to say because this was the first time they had talked since the party a few weeks ago? That was the most they had ever talked. Elizabeth even offered her a seat at their lunch table. Okay, maybe comparing herself to a rattlesnake wasn't enticing, but still. She extended herself. She held out her hand, and Emily left her hanging. The next few weeks, they went back to their usual routines. Sitting side by side in class, not speaking unless they had to. Eating lunch at different tables. Acting like they hadn't shared something important.

"Why don't we talk it over, then you do the writing and I'll do the artwork. Does that sound fair?" asked Elizabeth.

"Sure."

Elizabeth waited a few seconds. Nothing.

"Well . . ." she led her. "What do you think about it?"

"Well," Emily began hesitantly, "she says she's the 'slightest in the house.' Based on the background information, maybe this means that she knows she's the smallest . . . not in actual size, although maybe she is, but more like she's the smallest in terms of worth. She matters the least."

"Okay," Elizabeth said as she grabbed her oversize messenger bag and plopped it on the desk. She retrieved her sketch pad, a hair tie, and a charcoal pencil. She dropped her bag to the floor, pulled her hair back into a high, tight ponytail, and began drawing.

"Well, I'm not so sure about the second stanza, but the next one is pretty straightforward. She doesn't speak unless spoken to, and when she does, she's soft-spoken. Being loud and noticed scares her, would embarrass her."

"Nice, Delgado. I'm with you." Elizabeth drew furiously now. "What about the last stanza?"

"'And if it had not been so far – / And any one I knew / Were going –' Hmm," Emily said. "Where do you think 'it' is?"

Elizabeth stopped drawing. "Heaven." She picked up her bag again and dug through it to find a bunch of colored pencils held together by a hair scrunchy. She selected a pink pencil.

"Heaven?" asked Emily.

"Yeah."

"Hmm. So if heaven weren't so far, or if someone she knew was going, then she would go with them? Like if someone she knew was dying, she would want to go, too?"

Elizabeth didn't respond. She kept drawing.

Emily read the rest of the stanza: " 'I had often thought / How noteless – I could die –' "

"She doesn't think anyone would notice if she died. That's how insignificant she is," Emily said, almost in a whisper.

"Maybe she's suicidal," added Elizabeth.

"What?"

" 'I had often thought.' That's what she says. She often thinks about her death and how no one would care. If she often thinks about it, she might be suicidal."

They stared at each other for a few uncomfortable seconds. Elizabeth looked down at her own paper and continued to draw. After a few minutes, she asked, "Want to see the picture? It's a draft. If you like it, I'll re-do it in more detail on larger paper."

Emily's eyes widened as she viewed the drawing.

Elizabeth wasn't sure if Emily was impressed or scared. She leaned over to explain it. After several minutes, Ms. Diaz walked over.

"So, how are things going?"

"Great," said Elizabeth.

Emily looked at Ms. Diaz but didn't say anything.

"Let me see," Ms. Diaz said. She picked up the sketch pad with Elizabeth's drawing. Her eyebrows lifted as she scanned the page. She closed her eyes and breathed deeply. *Not again.*

On the top part of the paper was an image of a girl sitting, her arms behind the chair, her wrists bound. Each of her ankles was tied to a chair leg. She was screaming and struggling against the ropes. A pink blindfold covered her eyes.

Below this image were two others. A small girl surrounded by giant-size men covered her face with her hands. Under this was written, "I was the slightest in the House . . . I never spoke—unless addressed." Next to this image was a similar one, except in this one, the giant-size men were talking to one another—some were laughing—while the little girl lay in a corner, in a pool of blood, a straight-edged razor near her lifeless hand. Next to this was written, "I had often thought How noteless—I could die."

"Elizabeth, I think we should talk about this later," said Ms. Diaz.

"Why? I did what you wanted us to do, and now I'm in trouble?"

"I didn't say you were in trouble. I'd like to talk to you about *this*," Ms. Diaz said and pointed to the dead girl in the picture.

"What about it? Have you read the poem? It fits."

"Yes, I've read the poem, Elizabeth. I know it fits. Still, I'd like to talk one-on-one, without an audience."

Elizabeth glanced around the room and saw that everyone had stopped what they were doing and stared at them.

"Well, I don't want to talk later," Elizabeth said.

"Fine, then you can go to Ms. Gilbert's office."

"What? Why?" Elizabeth sprang up in her seat and glared at Ms. Diaz.

"Because you don't want to talk to me later, and I'm not going to argue with you now."

"But I don't want to talk to Ms. Gilbert," said Elizabeth. "Fine, I'll talk about it with you. You're the one who has a problem with it. Go ahead, talk!"

Students stared. Emily sank into her seat and raised her hand to cover her face.

"Elizabeth, I need you to lower your voice and calm down," said Ms. Diaz.

"I'm not yelling! I am calm! I'm just confused. I haven't done anything wrong. I did what you wanted us to do, and now I'm in trouble?" Her hands moved and her ponytail bobbed as she spoke.

"Elizabeth . . ." Tommy called her. When she looked at him, he shook his head intentionally from side to side. "Don't do this" was the message.

"Ms. Diaz, I think I can settle this," said Kevin. "I think Davis just needs to 'hug it out.'"

"Please, Kevin, not now," Ms. Diaz said, raising a hand to

him. "Elizabeth, I think the best thing would be for you to see Ms. Gilbert now. I'll call and tell her you're on your way."

Ms. Diaz crossed the room to reach the phone. Elizabeth stuffed her pencils and notebook into her bag. She stood up with force. Her chair slid back and her desk banged into Emily's.

"This is fucking bullshit," she said as she walked toward the door.

Tommy cringed. Emily gasped. The other students were genuinely shocked. They swear all the time with each other, but this crossed the line. Ms. Diaz hung up with Ms. Gilbert and dialed the assistant principal next.

As Elizabeth walked past Ms. Diaz, the two locked gazes. A few seconds after Elizabeth left, everyone in the classroom heard: bang, bang, bang. Ms. Diaz stepped into the hallway, the phone still against her ear. She saw a dent in a nearby locker and Elizabeth running and shaking her hand. When she turned back into the classroom, Emily was standing right in front of her.

"Can I go to the bathroom, please?"

"Sure," said Ms. Diaz.

Emily walked swiftly and then broke into a jog. She saw Elizabeth ahead of her. She had stopped running and stood with her back against a wall, one arm cradled by the other. Tears streamed down her face. Emily stood in front of Elizabeth, but didn't say anything.

"What do you want, Delgado?"

Emily reached into her pocket and pulled out a small package of tissues. She reached for Elizabeth's injured hand, turned it over gently, and pressed the plastic pack into her palm. Elizabeth closed her fingers around it, winced, and said, "Thanks."

Emily turned Elizabeth's hand back over and passed her thumb over Elizabeth's bruised knuckles.

"You're not like the girl in the poem," Emily said.

"That's not true."

"Really?" Emily asked and titled her head like a dog when it hears a strange noise.

"Really."

"But you live out loud."

"And all that gets me is suspended."

"You were challenged and you stood your ground," Emily said, raising her voice. "You wrestled with her and you won. You were Jacob."

"What the hell are you talking about, Delgado?"

Emily laughed but didn't explain.

Elizabeth pulled a tissue from the pack and wiped her face.

They stood in the hallway and stared at each other. Emily held a hand up, pushed her index finger down as if she were taking a picture, and said, "Click."

Elizabeth inhaled sharply.

Emily leaned in and whispered, "I *see* you, Elizabeth Davis." And then she walked away.

Behind her, Emily heard three more bangs—Elizabeth's fist hitting metal—and the assistant principal's voice shouting for her to stop and come with him to the office.

Emily stood outside Ms. Diaz's door. She rubbed the back of her neck, smoothed down her shirt, and buried her hands in her pockets to stop them from shaking.

When Emily walked through the door, everyone turned to look at her. She smiled politely and headed for her seat. Ms. Diaz crossed the room in a few quick steps and stood in front of her.

"Emily, are you okay?" she asked in a hushed tone.

Without hesitation, she said, "Yes, I'm fine."

CHAPTER 20

"That Distance was between Us"

Later that day, Emily shuffled behind Abby and Sarah in the lunch line as they described Elizabeth's meltdown to students who didn't witness it firsthand. She half listened to them as she added lettuce, carrots, and cucumbers to a Styrofoam plate. She had quit cross-country and pretty much stopped running altogether. No running meant no pasta at lunch.

"You know, you could eat more if you started running with us again. 'Exercise gives you endorphins. Endorphins make you happy,'" Abby said, quoting a movie they watched once.

"Ranch dressing makes me happy," said Emily. She dipped a baby carrot in a plastic cup half-filled with dressing and popped it into her mouth. "Plus, I always hated running in the cold. Maybe I'll try an indoor sport."

Abby shrugged and inched closer to the cashier. While Emily waited in line, she spotted Tommy and Kevin already seated in the cafeteria. After paying, she followed Sarah and Abby to their regular table but didn't sit down.

"What are you doing?" asked Sarah.

Emily stared at Kevin, who smiled and signaled to an empty chair.

"Kevin's waving me over," said Emily.

"Go ahead and talk to him. We'll save your seat," said Abby.

"I think I'll sit over there today," Emily said quietly.

"Really?" asked Abby. "Well, I guess Ranch dressing isn't the only thing that makes you happy."

Emily grinned. "Well, there's an extra seat over there."

"And, what happens when Elizabeth comes back?" asked Abby.

"I don't know," said Emily. "I'll probably come back here."

"Probably?" asked Abby.

"Leave her alone," said Sarah. "Go ahead, Em. Sit with your boyfriend. We'll be here, same place, same time every day."

"Of course," said Abby. "Don't get me wrong, I've been in on this romance since the very beginning."

"What does that mean?" asked Emily.

"It means I'm a big fan of 'Kevily,' but you've spent every weekend with Mr. Wonderful and now he's eating into our lunch time," Abby said with a smile. "I'm just saying don't forget about us little people."

Emily hesitated but didn't say anything.

"Ignore her and go," said Sarah. "Your salad's wilting and you're running out of time."

Emily gripped her lunch tray so hard, her knuckles turned white. Her heart raced as she maneuvered around students to Kevin and Tommy's table. She slid her body into the empty chair and her cold, sweaty hand into Kevin's steady grip. At the same time, a sophomore named Olivia slid into Emily's usual spot next to Sarah and opposite Abby.

Elizabeth sat silently in the passenger seat of her mom's car as they headed home. Mom had picked up Elizabeth from school and then taken her to the doctor's office to check the damage done to her hand.

When she got into the car at school, Elizabeth's mom had said, "Please don't say anything. I'm too angry to talk to you right now."

Hours later, Elizabeth flexed and curled her fingers, inspecting the Ace bandage on her hand. Mom focused on the traffic ahead or gazed out of the driver's side window then finally, broke the silence.

"What on earth possessed you to swear at a teacher?" her mom asked.

"It wasn't an earthly being, Julia," Elizabeth said.

"What?" she asked, glancing at Elizabeth while she drove.

"I was temporarily taken over by an alien. Swearing is illegal on her planet, so she wanted to try it out real quick before returning to the mother ship," said Elizabeth.

"You think this is funny?" Mom asked, raising her voice. "This is not funny. Since school started, you have skipped class, fallen from a tree, sprained your knee, cursed at a teacher, bruised your knuckles, and received a three-day in-school suspension. What's next? Expulsion? Juvenile detention? Is that what you want? To become an actual criminal sitting in jail and have your mother be a total basket case?"

"No."

"What was that?"

"I said, 'no,'" Elizabeth said louder.

"Oh, I thought you were being a smart-ass again."

"Not this time. Shocking, huh?" Elizabeth gazed out the window at the clear-blue, late-autumn sky. The shedding trees were a colorful blur as her mother sped along the roads. Elizabeth put her window down, closed her eyes, and leaned her head out of the car to let chilled gusts slap her in the face.

"Close the window, Elizabeth. It's getting cold in here."

"It's refreshing," Elizabeth countered, but she closed the window anyway. "Imagine that, we disagree on something."

"You know what, Elizabeth? I am tired of your attitude. Do you think we could ever have a real conversation if you're always being sarcastic?"

"Is this supposed to be a real conversation? It sounds more like a lecture to me."

"Fine, then let it be a lecture, which means stop with

the back talk and listen," her mom said. "Your behavior is unacceptable. Not only is it reckless, it's selfish. You don't consider how your words and actions affect other people. How do you think Ms. Diaz felt today? You were completely disrespectful. You ruined her class.

"How do you think I felt when your principal called? Do you know how embarrassing it is to be told that your child cursed at the teacher and dented some lockers with her fist? You weren't raised to believe that it's okay to act that way.

"And what about your partner for this assignment? How are you supposed to work with her if you're serving a three-day internal suspension?

"Plus, do you realize that every time you pull one of your little stunts, I have to leave work, which means I lose hours and earn less money. And then, because you always seem to hurt yourself, I have to take you to the doctor, which costs money."

"You missed the turn," Elizabeth said.

"What?"

"You missed the turn. You were too busy lecturing me."

"Damn it," her mom said. She pulled over, made a U-turn when she could, and then took the turn she had missed.

The two were quiet again for a few minutes.

"So, do you have anything to say?" her mom asked. "And it better not be one of your clever little comments."

"I'll apologize to Ms. Diaz," Elizabeth said.

"You should apologize to the whole class," her mom suggested.

"Fine, I'll apologize to the class. My partner and I are splitting the work, so we don't have to be together to get it done, and I'll pay you back somehow for the doctor's visits."

"All of that is great, but you're missing the point, Elizabeth."

"Which is?"

"You need to pull yourself together before something horrible happens," her mom said. "When you go to school, I want you to attend class, do your work, get good grades, and stay out of trouble."

Her mom parked the car in their driveway, turned off the engine, and faced Elizabeth.

"Is that clear?" she asked.

"Yes."

"You're grounded until further notice," she added.

"Fine."

"And I want your phone."

"Here." Elizabeth grabbed her cell from her bag and handed it to her mother. She turned away from her mom and looked out the passenger side window. She sat still, cradling her injured hand in the other, her thumb rubbing the bandage.

"Does it hurt?" her mom asked gently.

"Yes," Elizabeth said. "Everything hurts."

"Yeah, I know the feeling."

Elizabeth turned to her mom. "Are you being sarcastic?"

"No, I'm not."

Elizabeth shoved the car door open, climbed out, and slammed it shut, leaving her mom alone in the car. As she dragged herself to the front door, she wiped away her tears with her sleeve.

Later that night, Emily texted Abby and Sarah: Hey, girls, I'm at Kevin's for dinner. The story is we all went to the library after school and now we're at Sarah's working on a project, okay?

Sarah: Sounds good. Have fun.

Abby: Doesn't sound good. Who does homework on a Friday night? Lame cover story, Em.

Emily: Well, I had to say something. Just remember in case you run into my parents sometime soon.

Abby: We'd have to hang out to possibly run into them.

Emily: Ugh! Abby, come on.

Abby: I'm just playing . . . Kinda . . . Have fun!

Emily shook her head and tucked her phone into her jeans pocket.

"You okay?" asked Kevin.

"Alpha Dog Abby just growled at me, so, you know, the usual," said Emily.

"It's because you sat with me at lunch. She's worried you'll break away from the pack and join some cooler wolves," Kevin said and then howled.

Emily laughed.

"Really, Kev, is that any way to behave when you're trying to impress someone?" asked George as he walked into the kitchen.

"We're already dating, Dad. I don't have to impress her anymore," Kevin said and winked at Emily.

George shook his head and said, "Be patient, Emily; he's got a lot to learn."

George rolled up his shirtsleeves and slid an apron over his head to protect his button-down shirt and black pants. He grabbed a few vegetables from the fridge and placed them on the counter. Emily responded to his movements by slipping on an apron and reaching for a nearby knife and waiting green pepper.

"Half or the whole thing?" she asked.

"Half is fine and then dump it into the sauce. Kevin, can you start boiling the water for the pasta? Thanks." George always asked, but he wasn't really asking. "I'm sorry we don't have something more elaborate, but it was a busy day."

"This is great," said Emily. After chopping for a few minutes, she asked, "So, how did you and John meet?"

"We first dated in college, but we didn't really get together until a few years after we graduated," George said as he minced cilantro. "He was one of those moody artist types in school, but he wasn't an artist. He was a business major."

"So, he was just moody," Emily said with a laugh.

"Basically," George said and smiled. "I tried to work around it, you know, and then one day I asked him, 'Do I make you happy?' and he said, 'Yes,' and that was *it*."

"That's so sweet." Emily dumped the green pepper pieces into the sauce, stirred, and then offered Kevin a taste.

"It needs garlic, Dad," he said.

Emily took over chopping the cilantro while George started on a clove of garlic.

"No, I mean that was *it*, as in I let him have it and we broke up."

"What? Why?"

"Because no one can make another person happy," said George. "He was happy when he was with me, but otherwise he wasn't. That's not enough. I mean, in a relationship, you have your ups and downs, sure, and you help each other through, but if a person is genuinely unhappy, it won't work. No amount of love or laughter from the other person can fix that. Each person has to love and laugh on their own. They need to feel it for real, deep down, in here."

George tucked his fist into his abdomen. Emily flattened her palm on her belly.

"In the stomach? Really, Dad? Don't ever think about writing Hallmark cards, okay?"

John walked into the kitchen with his suit jacket over his arm and a hand pulling at his tie. He patted Kevin on the back and said, "He's not telling our story again, is he?"

"She asked for it," said Kevin.

"So what changed?" asked Emily.

"I did," said John. "And once I did, we got together and the rest is history. The end."

"You are the worst storyteller ever," said George.

"I like to cut to the chase," said John. "Plus, I'm hungry. Let's eat."

"It's almost ready. Can you and Kevin set the table? Thanks." George then whispered to Emily, "We'll talk more later."

After dinner, Kevin challenged Emily to video game baseball.

"That's not fair," said Emily. "Baseball's your sport. We have to play something neutral, like tennis."

"Fine, tennis it is. Prepare to lose."

"I don't think so," said Emily.

Kevin yelled like Serena Williams whenever he hit the virtual ball over the net. Emily taunted the refs like John McEnroe whenever Kevin scored a point. During the final match, Emily dived and swung at the same time. When she pulled her hand back, she clocked Kevin in the face with her nunchuk.

"Oh my God, I'm so sorry," Emily said, but she was laughing too hard to sound sincere. Kevin laughed, too, and collapsed on the couch, calling a much-needed time-out.

"You know, tennis isn't supposed to be a contact sport," he said, rubbing his face.

"I'm sorry," she said and kissed his cheek where she had hit him. "I got carried away."

"It's okay." He smiled and then looked at her seriously. "I hope my dad's relationship advice earlier didn't bother you."

"Why would it?"

"Em, I may not be on the honor roll, but I'm not stupid."

"What are you talking about?"

Kevin pulled Emily toward him. She turned so that she sat with her back against his chest, his arms wrapped around her.

"I know you're happy when we're together, but . . ."

"Kevin . . ."

"Let me finish," he whispered. "I've got lots of love and laughter, and it's all for you, Em, but I know something is going on with you. So, if you want or need me to do something, I will, okay?"

"Okay," said Emily. She closed her eyes and gripped his arms, but she couldn't talk about it. Could she even explain it, find the right words, if she wanted to? So, instead, she turned toward him and forced a grin. "I need you to answer three questions for me. That will make me feel better."

"Okay, shoot."

"Have you really dated most of the sophomore class?"

"No."

"Did you sleep with a high school girl when you were in eighth grade?"

"No. Would it matter if I said yes? Would you feel differently about me?"

"No. Just curious."

"What's the third question?" he asked.

"Will you drop out of high school and join the circus with me?"

"Yes," he said. He pulled her close again. "We could be clowns or ride elephants or do something dangerous like walking the tightrope without a net."

"Being a clown or riding elephants would be okay, but I couldn't do the tightrope." She pulled his arms tighter around her and added in a whisper, "I need a net."

CHAPTER 21

Letter #2

Dear Ms. Diaz,

I'm sorry about what happened in class on Friday. I know you didn't like the drawing, but you didn't give us a chance to explain. Anyway, better late than never. Here goes: Society tied the girl to the chair. "They" covered her eyes, so she doesn't experience the world completely. She's a blinded, caged animal screaming in frustration. Haven't you ever felt that way? Like you're being held down and you want to break free?

The picture is black and white because the gender issue was black and white then: Men were superior. Women were inferior. Period. The blindfold is pink. Get the symbolism? I assumed you'd like that. It's actually a reference to a No Doubt song called "Just a Girl." Do you know it? It was out in the '90s. That's when you were young, right? Well, at least younger. The song reminded us of Dickinson and how women were held back by society. That picture is based on the background information you gave us. The other two are based on the poem. The girl is small in size because she's unimportant in her male-dominated world. She's so unimportant, she dies and no one notices.

Come on, it totally works. If you had let us explain, maybe things wouldn't have gotten ugly. You might not like the drawing, but it's a slam-dunk A+. Didn't you tell us once in class we might not like everything we read or do in class, but we should be open-minded?

Ms. Diaz made a copy for herself and another for Ms. Gilbert. This time the note read, *Suzanne, another letter from Elizabeth. She's begging for a reaction, so she's going to get it. I'll keep you posted.*

Dear Elizabeth,

This might be awkward, having me write to you, but I need to explain a few things after what happened in class. I liked your drawing, and yes, it does fit the poem. I get it: the girl tied down by society yearning to break free. The pink ribbon, while the rest is black and white—very clever. Really. Great interpretation. It's not because

I disliked your picture that I wanted to talk to you—I'm concerned that you see yourself as the girl in the chair, being tied down and frustrated, or worse, as the girl in the corner.

Can I help in any way? If I can, I will.

Sincerely,

Ms. Diaz

CHAPTER 22

"We talked as Girls do –"

On Monday, Emily walked alone in a near-empty hallway with her arms crossed, as if she were hugging herself.

"Hi, Emily," Ms. Diaz called out.

Emily snapped out of her daze.

"Oh, hi."

"Are you okay?" Ms. Diaz asked as she stood in front of Emily. "We had a tough class Friday. I'm sorry you were in the middle of that."

"I'm fine," said Emily. "I was surprised and, well, a little embarrassed, but I'm okay."

"You know, despite what happened, I still think you two can learn from each other. I wanted to tell you that I paired you up for a reason, beyond your writing and her drawing abilities. Elizabeth takes chances, although obviously she can get carried away sometimes."

They both laughed.

"But, you tend to be cautious," said Ms. Diaz. "You're a great student, Emily, but your work is almost too neat. Your writing is mechanically perfect, but it lacks voice."

"Voice?"

"I can't hear you on paper, Emily," she said. "I know, without looking at the name, when I'm reading Elizabeth's work or Tommy's or even Kevin's. Their personalities are on the page. They have a voice when they write. Does that make sense?"

"Yeah," she whispered. "I'll work on that."

"If you want me to read a rough draft or need an extension, let me know." Ms. Diaz smiled and walked away. After a few moments, Emily said, "Thanks, Ms. D," but she didn't hear her.

Ms. Diaz continued on to the small in-school suspension room. Elizabeth sat bent over a desk, arms stacked under her face to serve as a pillow, her messenger bag anchored on the floor next to her feet.

Ms. Diaz waved at Mr. Wilson, who was nicknamed "The Warden," and then said, "Hi, Elizabeth."

No answer.

Ms. Diaz grabbed a nearby chair and sat opposite Elizabeth, who stirred but didn't raise her head.

"Elizabeth?" Ms. Diaz said louder and reached over to shake the girl's arm a little.

Elizabeth finally lifted her head, one eye still closed.

"Did you get the note I slipped into your locker?"

"Yes," Elizabeth said.

"I was hoping we could talk."

"No offense, Ms. D, but I ended up here after our last conversation. I don't feel like talking to you."

"That's fair, but I'd still like to talk to you."

"All right, talk," Elizabeth said, holding her head up with a hand on her cheek.

"You look tired."

"Thanks. You look great, too." Elizabeth put her head back down.

"Are you getting enough sleep?"

"Obviously not," Elizabeth said, head still down.

"Why not?"

Elizabeth whipped her head up.

"Is this really what you want to talk about? Why I'm not sleeping? It has nothing to do with literature or poetry or your favorite female recluse. So, why do you care?"

"Watch your tone, Miss Davis," said Mr. Wilson.

"Thanks, Chris, but it's okay."

"Holler if you need me," he added.

Ms. Diaz turned back to Elizabeth. "I don't know why. I just do," she said.

Both sat silent for a while.

"You're not going away, are you?" asked Elizabeth.

"No. So, why aren't you sleeping well?"

"I want to ask you a question," said Elizabeth. "Why did you become a teacher?"

"Because I love literature. That's the short explanation."

"Interesting," said Elizabeth. "You didn't say anything about your students."

Ms. Diaz didn't respond.

"So, do you really care?" Elizabeth asked.

Ms. Diaz hesitated and then said softly, "Yes."

The bell rang.

"I'll see you later," Ms. Diaz said before she left. Elizabeth watched her go and then put her head down on her arms and dozed off.

After school, once the buses cleared out, Elizabeth cut across the grass to the nearby wooded area. She was almost where she fell from the tree when she noted swishing leaves and snapping twigs behind her.

"Who's there?" she yelled as she spun around. The movement stopped.

"If you don't show yourself right now, I will beat you to a bloody pulp," she announced.

The sounds of someone walking through the woods started again. Elizabeth's heart raced and she balled her hands into fists. She lowered her messenger bag to the ground in case she had to run.

"Relax, Davis, you're not in *The Hunger Games*," Emily said as she became visible from the trees and walked toward Elizabeth.

"What are you doing here, Delgado?" asked Elizabeth with a mix of relief and annoyance.

"I saw you walking this way and was curious," she said.

"So, you're following me. That's creepy."

"What are you doing?" asked Emily.

"I'm returning to the scene of the crime. This is where I hurt my knee the first time. I think it knows because it's twitching with pain." Elizabeth leaned over and touched her knee with her fingertips. She wore jeans and a long, dark gray T-shirt with Georgia O'Keeffe's "Summer Days" printed across the front. Over her T-shirt, she wore a black hooded sweatshirt, zipped partway, hood up.

Emily laughed and walked past Elizabeth.

"Where are you going?"

"Like I said, I'm curious. Come on."

The two stopped once they were deep into the woods, much farther than where Elizabeth fell. The trees here were broad, tall, and numerous. Bright autumn sunlight pierced through the branches in interesting angles, like mini-spotlights from the sky. In the center of this area was a small clearing, a place where a few trees didn't grow. There was enough room for a person to lie down comfortably, so Elizabeth did. She crossed her legs at her ankles, closed her eyes, and rested her arms away from her body, palms up.

After a few moments, she opened one eye and caught Emily staring at her.

"Listen, Delgado, if you're going to chill here, sit down and stop worrying about getting your designer clothes dirty."

Emily smiled and lowered herself to the ground.

"It's beautiful, isn't it?" said Elizabeth.

For several minutes, they observed the surrounding nature. Leaves of varied hues fluttered to the ground, while the evergreens stood tall, full of themselves, like a group of confident teenagers huddled together, talking and throwing their hair back slightly when an occasional breeze blew by.

Elizabeth sat up and dug out a package of Pop-Tarts from her messenger bag. She turned to face Emily and handed her one.

"So, I'm looking at your hair and I remembered something," Emily said, breaking the silence. Elizabeth squinted her eyes and braced for what she figured was coming— questions about how she looked before, why she changed, what happened. Instead, Emily said, "When I was little, I hated washing my hair, so one day I dumped all of the shampoo into the toilet and put the cap back on the bottle, so my mom wouldn't notice. The problem was, I didn't flush the toilet, and our dog drank out of the bowl. He walked right into my mom with suds all over his snout."

Elizabeth snorted a laugh and shook her head.

"Once, my sister was helping my mom with the groceries. She dropped a soda bottle, but didn't say anything and put it into the fridge. Well, a few minutes later, I opened the fridge and grabbed the soda, but did she warn me? Of course not. I opened the bottle and the soda erupted like a volcano. My mom was shouting, 'Get out of my kitchen.' We ran outside and laughed so hard it hurt."

"That's funny." Emily mentally scanned her memories.

"When I was little, I was afraid of the dark, so I used to sleep with a pile of stuffed animals. There were so many, you couldn't see me. I still have a stuffed dog I named Abercrombie way before I knew anything about the clothing store. I know it's silly, but I can't part with him."

Elizabeth didn't hesitate. "I hate thunderstorms. I used to run into my mom and dad's room and jump into their bed. My mom would sing lullabies to calm me down. Now, when a storm passes, I put in my earbuds and listen to music."

"Punk?"

"No, classical."

"Cool." Emily hesitated and then said, "My parents want me to see a doctor because I'm always tired and I ache all over like I have arthritis. They think something's wrong with me."

"You might be anemic or have a vitamin deficiency or something," said Elizabeth.

"Maybe."

Elizabeth took a deep breath. "Last year, my father left us. He fell in love with another woman, a family friend who was also married. I found out because I caught them kissing in his car near Rogers Park. At first, I froze, but then something snapped inside me. I ran to the front of the car at an angle, leaped on the hood, and started jumping up and down.

"When my dad got out of the car, I dived on him. We landed on the street and I started hitting him. After a while, he wrapped his arms around me, like he was hugging me, and he let me flail until I was spent. He kept saying, 'I'm sorry, Elizabeth. I'm sorry.' I told him to shut up. I turned away from him and crawled to the sidewalk. He reached out to me, but I kicked his hand and told him I hated him and to leave me alone. Part of me wanted him to get away from me, but another part of me wanted him to pick me up like I was three and tell me everything was going to be okay, that he would fix everything."

"What did he do?" asked Emily.

"He did what I told him to do. He left. We don't talk anymore. He tries, but . . ." Elizabeth shook her head. "And my mom pretty much hates me. I don't blame her. So, my parents want me to see a doctor, too."

"Why?"

"Really, Delgado?" she said with a laugh as she wiped her tear-streaked face with the sleeves of her hoodie.

"Yeah, well, maybe something is wrong with you," Emily said with a smile. "I'm sorry. I knew your parents weren't together, but I didn't know the details."

Elizabeth nibbled on her Pop-Tart. After a while, she said, "I'm sorry about Friday."

"Okay," said Emily.

And they sat on the ground in comfortable silence, letting colored leaves and the cool wind hit them, until their Pop-Tarts were gone and the late bus arrived to take them home.

CHAPTER 23

My Letter to the World

Going to the doctor was less of a nightmare than I expected. He asked lots of questions: Are you sleeping too much or too little? Do you have headaches or other physical pains? Is your energy level low? Is it hard to make decisions? Do you feel like a failure? Has your appetite increased or decreased? Have you considered self harm or suicide?

I answered most of his questions honestly. He knew I had lost weight, since the first thing they always do is throw you on a scale. I told him my mental state would improve if the world weren't so concerned about body image. He didn't laugh. Not even a grin. Oh well. I hadn't lost the weight intentionally.

When the doctor asked if I had felt this way for more than two weeks, I laughed out loud. He didn't think it was funny. He prescribed an antidepressant and gave my mom a list of therapists to call. There was no way I'd talk to a shrink; she couldn't force me. My parents agreed I should start with the pills, and then they argued for hours on the phone about whose fault it was. For the rest of the day, my mom stared at me and talked in short, baby-like sentences, as if anything more would break me.

The prescription wasn't a solution, but a first step to . . . what? Normalcy? No. That would be asking too much. Feeling better? Maybe. Who knows? I read the fine print about the possible side effects—everything from a mild headache to increased suicidal thoughts, especially in young people. So, taking the pills could magically cure me or make matters entirely worse? Brilliant.

I didn't take one the first morning I was supposed to, but I brought it to school, rubbed it with my thumb and forefinger like a worry stone. Could it really work? Or would it be like taking aspirin and when the medicine wears off, the pain returns? In that case, wouldn't I have to take these forever? And wouldn't that be like wearing a mask for the rest of my life? On the outside, I'd be smiling, laughing, but what was going on underneath?

I wanted to talk to someone—not a shrink, but maybe you—about all of this, but I couldn't. I knew you'd have to report it to someone else. It's not your job to fix me. And then, there'd be meetings with counselors and social workers and psychologists and psychiatrists. And all of them would want to know the same thing, "What's wrong?" and they'd stare at me, waiting for an explanation.

So, I pretended to take the pills and never talked about it to anyone after that day at the doctor's, not even you, Ms. Diaz, although you probably would have understood.

CHAPTER 24

"'Tis so appalling— it exhilarates"

Emily walked beside Sarah and Abby as they made their way to first period. Sarah and Abby exchanged glances. Sarah had a questioning look on her face; Abby rolled her eyes.

Sarah hooked her arm around Emily's elbow and leaned into her a little as they walked.

"So, we're ready to do some Christmas shopping. Want to join us?" asked Sarah.

"Sure. When, though, because I promised to help Kevin with his shopping, too."

"Kevin can survive without you for an afternoon," said Abby. "We need some girl time."

"Yeah, Em, we miss you," said Sarah.

Emily offered a weak smile. "I know. I've been busy . . ."

"You don't have more to do than anyone else," said Abby. "If you're going to stay with Kevin, you have to learn how to fit us in. We were here first and we'll be here if you guys break up."

"Jeez, Abby," said Sarah.

"What? It's true. If you cut off your friends when you're dating someone, you'll be all alone if the relationship ends."

"And I wonder why she's cutting us off, Abby? Maybe it's because you have no filter between your brain and your mouth," said Sarah.

"What? We've talked about this kind of stuff a million times during sleepovers. I thought we all agreed that we'd stick together when we dated people. I'm not trying to be mean. You get that, right, Em?"

"Good morning, ladies," Ms. Diaz said as the girls reached her classroom.

"Good morning," Sarah and Abby said cheerily.

"Emily, are you okay?" Ms. Diaz asked. "You look a little pale."

"I think I have a cold or something. I don't know." Emily shrugged and circled a piece of hair around her ear.

"Well, I hope you feel better."

"Thanks." Emily walked into the room behind Abby and Sarah, but stopped and added quietly, "I haven't finished the essay yet. May I have an extension?"

"Sure. Give me the paper on Monday. If you're still not feeling well, hand it in whenever you can. You've never asked for an extension before, so I'm fine with that," said Ms. Diaz.

"Okay, thanks."

When Elizabeth approached, Ms. Diaz said, "Welcome back." It was her first day in class since her internal suspension.

"Thanks," Elizabeth said with a grin. She carried an art portfolio along with her usual book bag. "May I present something for extra credit? You said we could, right?"

"Yes. Students presented yesterday, but since you weren't in class, you can share today."

"Thanks."

The rest of the students shuffled in and sat down.

"All right, class, before we get to what I have planned, Elizabeth is going to present her work since she wasn't here yesterday. Emily, are you joining her?"

Emily's eyes widened and her mouth opened and shut, like a fish trying to breathe out of water.

"No," Elizabeth answered. Emily looked relieved. "We're working on the parts separately, and this is sort of about what we did but sort of not."

"Okay, your vague description makes me a little nervous," said Ms. Diaz.

Elizabeth grinned as she carried her portfolio to the front of the room. She unzipped the case and gently pulled out a large final draft of the sketch she worked on in class the previous week. She carefully attached the drawing to the easel Ms. Diaz used for her flip chart. She also retrieved note cards with writing on them.

For the first time, the whole class saw what sparked the argument between Ms. Diaz and Elizabeth: The screaming girl, her wrists bound, her ankles tied to the chair legs. The pink blindfold, the lone color in the dark scene created with black charcoal. The two other images of giant men surrounding a small girl who dies unnoticed.

Students stared wide-eyed. Tommy nodded in approval.

"Whoa, Davis," said Kevin, breaking the silence. "Creepy, but I like it. It's disturbing and beautiful at the same time. Kind of like you."

Students laughed.

Elizabeth glared at Kevin. He expected a snarky comeback, but instead she agreed with him.

"Exactly. ' 'Tis so appalling – it exhilarates.' "

"What?" Kevin asked.

"The picture is about the poem Emily and I worked on, but that line is from another poem. Before I go any further, though, I promised my mother I'd apologize to the class for my behavior last week. She's going to e-mail you, Ms. D, to confirm that I did, so here I am saying publicly: I'm sorry for disrupting the class and for being disrespectful."

"Thank you for apologizing," said Ms. Diaz.

"But, I'm not sorry for what I drew," she added.

"All right. Explain."

"Well, I did a little research. At first, I looked for interpretations of the poem we got last week. I wanted to get a new idea for the visual part that would be less disturbing. But as I looked around, I discovered something." Elizabeth paused. "Emily Dickinson had a dark side. I mean, I don't know if she had a dark side in her real life, but she wrote some dark poems. They aren't all about chestnuts and bumblebees. She wrote a lot about death and pain."

Elizabeth reviewed her note cards. "Like, one poem, number 335, starts: ' 'Tis not that Dying hurts us so – / 'Tis Living – hurts us more –.' Most people are afraid of death, and probably of dying a painful death, but this line says life, with all of its daily drama, is more painful.

"Poem number 281, the one that starts ' 'Tis so appalling – it exhilarates –,' is one of her Gothic poems. At first I wondered, how can something be appalling and exhilarating at the same time? But then I realized, we pay money to watch horror movies, and we slow down to stare at car accidents. Why? Because they're frightening and fascinating at the same time."

Elizabeth flipped to another note card. "She's got lots of cool, disturbing comparisons, too. One example is 'My Life had stood – a Loaded Gun –.' Another is 'A still – Volcano – Life – / That flickered in the night –.' Life equals a loaded gun. Life equals a still volcano. Loaded guns eventually go off. Volcanoes erupt.

"She even wrote one about suicide. At the end of poem number 1062, the person in the poem 'Caressed a Trigger absently / And wandered out of Life.' "

Elizabeth paused again and scanned the room. Most students stared directly at her. Emily and a few others wrote in their notebooks. Ms. Diaz nodded for her to continue.

"Finally, I noticed she often uses exclamation points."

"You go from suicide to punctuation marks?" Kevin asked. "So she was excited? Whoa, that *is* dark."

Elizabeth glared at Kevin.

"Ignore him," Ms. Diaz said. "Go on."

"Maybe she was excited in some of them, but all of those exclamation points made me think . . . well, I know you told us we can't assume everything a writer produces is about her own life . . . but when I saw those exclamation points, I thought . . ."

Ms. Diaz gradually moved forward from the back of the room to stand a few feet away from Elizabeth. The girl turned her head and focused on Ms. Diaz instead of the waiting students.

"What did you think?" asked Ms. Diaz.

"That maybe she understood."

"Understood what?"

"Anger. Maybe she got pissed off, too. And not a little mad, but furious, like if a monster's inside you, squeezing your lungs so you can't breathe and pounding you right between the eyes with its fist."

The class held its collective breath, waiting for their teacher's response.

"And, Ms. Gilbert knows all about this?"

"Yes," Elizabeth said and shifted from one foot to the other.

"Okay. Continue." Ms. Diaz strolled to her previous spot in the back of the room.

"After reading some of these other poems, I came back to the poem Emily and I read," said Elizabeth. "And, it definitely had an underlying tone of resentment. My picture is disturbing, but I think it fits the poem perfectly. I mean, the person in the poem thinks she matters so little that her death would go unnoticed. *That's* disturbing.

"So, I didn't change the picture. I'm hoping the additional research and extra credit will make up for any points I'll lose for not changing the picture."

The class was quiet for a moment, waiting.

"The end," Elizabeth said, unsure of how to finish the presentation.

Her classmates and Ms. Diaz laughed in response.

"Well done," said Ms. Diaz.

"Really?"

"Yes."

"I'm not in trouble?"

"No."

"Sweet!" Elizabeth walked to her seat with a genuine smile on her face.

Next to her, Emily shut her notebook to hide what she wrote inside:

Living hurts us more . . .

My life—a loaded gun . . . When will it go off?

A still volcano . . . When will it erupt?

When the bell rang, Elizabeth let the class empty and then approached Ms. Diaz's desk. She opened her bag and pulled out a shoe box that was bent in a few places and completely wrapped in duct tape.

"Here, this is for you," said Elizabeth.

Ms. Diaz turned the box over, eyes squinted in confusion.

"Thanks. What is it exactly?"

"A bunch of my stuff, poems and drawings mostly. I want you to have them."

"Aren't they important to you?"

"Yeah."

"Then why are you giving them away?"

Elizabeth shrugged.

"Can I read them?" asked Ms. Diaz.

"Not yet. I'll tell you when."

Elizabeth turned toward the door.

"Wait," said Ms. Diaz. She grabbed a black binder from her bookshelf, wiped off a visible layer of dust, and wrapped masking tape around it several times.

"There." She placed it next to Elizabeth's box.

"What's that?"

"A writing project I set aside when someone I loved died suddenly. Nothing mattered since she was gone. I keep promising myself I'll finish it, but year after year the binder sits here and collects dust. The tape is a formality."

She stared at the binder and shoe box for a second and then added, "I'll tear off the tape and finally do something with it when you're ready to share yours. No pressure. Whenever. I'll be ready when you are."

"Okay." Elizabeth headed toward the door but stopped and spun around. "Ms. D, can I ask you something? You seem fine now. How did you get there?"

"After a while, something clicked inside me. It's hard to explain, but at that moment, I was ready to let some things go and move forward."

"Something clicks?" Elizabeth asked.

"Yeah. You'll know. That's the beginning of a long process." Ms. Diaz pressed her palm on the center of her binder. "I'm not entirely fine yet. I'm still waiting for a couple of things to click."

Unsure of what to say, Elizabeth was about to walk out when Ms. Diaz said, "I'm curious about the pink blindfold reference. No Doubt is a little old for you, aren't they?"

Elizabeth grinned. "My dad left a few of his CDs behind."

"He left an awful lot behind," said Ms. Diaz. "I'm sure he misses . . . everything."

"You really think so?"

Ms. Diaz nodded.

Elizabeth grinned and then bolted out of the room, wiping her eyes with her shirtsleeves.

CHAPTER 25

Letter #3

DECEMBER

Dear Ms. Diaz,

It's Christmastime. I'm grateful for all I have, yet I'm dreading being home for almost two weeks. That's all.

Dear Elizabeth,

You're a smart, talented girl. If you find these days off from school unbearable, and you need to get away from your family, then do that. Go outside and discover something beautiful. Take pictures, draw, or write poetry. Do something. Sitting and thinking too much will make matters worse. I hope this helps.

Sincerely,

Ms. Diaz

CHAPTER 26

"To try to speak, and miss the way"

The Delgados sat in their ornate, candlelit dining room, silverware and china clinking on dinner plates as sweet potatoes, roasted ham, and *pasteles* made their way around the table. Water, wine, and *coquito* generously spilled into waiting crystal glasses.

Pop and Mamá balanced the table, sitting at opposite ends, with Austin and Tía Liana on one side and Emily on the other.

"So, how's the school year, Sis?" asked Austin. He looked a lot like Pop: tall and broad-shouldered with thick, dark hair and a Hollywood smile. They both looked intently at whoever was talking, as if whatever was being said was the most important thing they had ever heard.

"Fine."

"Her grades are down," said Pop. "She never handed in an essay in English. I check your grades online, you know."

"I know," said Emily. "And my teacher gave me an extension on the paper."

"I'm sure it wasn't an indefinite extension. And she has a B+ in Spanish, of all things. *¿Pueden creerlo?*"

"Give her a break, Eddie," said Tía Liana, the only person who got away with using her little brother's childhood nickname.

Emily grinned at Tía Liana. She was a perpetual student who was now pursuing a doctorate in fine arts. Always outspoken and spunky, she was quick to pick up her ankle-length peasant skirt and kick off her shoes to chase Emily and Austin around the house when they were younger. She painted with similar abandon, which is why splashes of color often streaked her clothes. Her brown, curly hair was usually tied back, high in a ponytail, so it didn't get in her way.

"Going to school is her job," Pop said. "We expect her to work hard and get good grades. Is that too much to ask?"

"No, but no one's perfect," said Tía Liana. "A B+ is a good grade, and she missed one essay in English. *¿Y qué?* She probably handed in fifty others on time."

"I'm in the top ten percent of my class," Emily said quietly.

"That's great, Em," said Austin.

"Your brother was valedictorian," said Pop.

"How could we forget?" Tía Liana lifted the glass plate of *pasteles*. "So much food, Eddie, it's a shame your mouth is empty. *Adelante, come más.*"

The others laughed.

"Sure, send them down, *Hermana*," he said, accepting the offer but ignoring the overt message to stop talking. Tía Liana winked at Emily.

"And you all wonder why I don't visit more often," said Austin with a smile. "Maybe we should talk about something less hostile on the eve of our savior's birth. How about those Red Sox, huh?"

"You know I'm a Yankees fan," said Pop. "And your comment reminds me, we are all going to midnight Mass tonight. I don't want any arguments. This one has been throwing a tantrum every Sunday."

"Oh, here we go," said Emily. She turned to her mother who was eating small bites of food and sipping her wine. "Mamá, are you going to say anything?"

"*¿Qué quieres que te diga?*" she asked.

"I don't know, something, anything to help me out here."

"You're old enough to fight your own battles," said Mamá.

Emily's breath caught short. She swallowed hard and said, "O-kay then, what about Austin? Does he attend church in Amherst?"

Austin shook his head and shot his sister the "*cállate la boca*" glare. He coughed before he said, "I go most Sundays."

"Not every Sunday? Does that really count then?" asked Emily.

"The *pasteles* are delicious, Em," Austin said. "You should eat more. You're a little *flaca*."

Everyone laughed.

"Saying grace tonight was probably the first time she's prayed in weeks," said Pop.

"How do you know that, Pop?" asked Emily. "I can pray anytime and anywhere I want."

" 'Some keep the Sabbath going to church. I keep it staying at home,' " said Austin.

"Who said that?" asked Emily.

"A famous female poet who stopped going to church," said Austin. "Come on, I go to Amherst College. You get one guess."

"Emily Dickinson," said Tía Liana. "That was way too easy."

"Okay, but she made the same point as you, Em; she didn't need traditional religion to be spiritual."

"Because 'The kingdom of God is within you,' " said Tía Liana.

"Who said that?" asked Austin.

"Jesus. It's also the title of a book by Tolstoy."

"Show off," Pop said and laughed.

"Well, I *was* valedictorian," she said with a smile. "Were you, Eddie? I don't remember."

"Emily, pass the *pasteles* to Tía," said Pop.

"No thanks. I'll fill my mouth with this instead." She lifted her glass of *coquito*. "Cheers, everyone."

They all raised and clinked their glasses.

"So, I've been thinking . . . ," Pop started.

"Good for you!" said Tía Liana.

Everyone snickered. "So, like I was saying, I've been thinking . . . about running for state representative."

Tía Liana jumped out of her seat to hug her brother. Austin and Emily followed, but Mamá stayed in her seat. When Emily returned to her place, she gripped the side of her chair with one hand and gulped her water with the other. Her pulse raced and small beads of sweat formed at her hairline.

"My party's behind me, *gracias a Dios*, but it's still going to be a lot of work," said Pop. "This will be a bigger campaign, so it'd have to be a team effort. Isabel will go out more, attend some charity functions and whatnot." Emily glanced at Mamá, who sat still and smiled without showing any teeth. "Austin, you better not get caught at any keg parties or participating in fraternity hazing or anything stupid like that. And Emily, you need to get your grades up and stay out of trouble. You remember what happened when you were caught drinking."

"How could I forget?"

"This isn't a joke, Emily. We are educated, moral Latinos who attend church and live by rock-solid family values."

"Is that what you believe or is that your campaign slogan?" asked Tía Liana.

"Both," he said. "My point is, my opponents will be ready to pounce. *¿Entienden?*"

"And what if they misstep? What then, Eddie?" asked Tía Liana.

"I don't know, maybe a military academy for Austin or a Catholic boarding school for Emily."

Tía Liana howled with laughter, but stopped when no one joined her.

"You're serious? Come on, Eddie." She turned to Emily's mom. "¿Isabel, *vas a decir algo?*"

"Yes," said Mamá. Emily held her breath and prayed her mom would say, *No más, Edwin. Your children need room to screw up. That's what kids do. That's what you did.* And then she'd spill some of his childhood slipups and he could never again pretend to be perfect or expect them to be.

Instead, she sighed and announced, "It's time for dessert."

Emily wanted to sprint from the table, but white flecks spotted her vision and she was certain she'd land facedown on the gleaming hardwood floors if she tried to stand.

The day after Christmas, Austin drove Emily to Abby's house for their annual gift-exchange-while-eating-leftovers ritual. Since Austin was on holiday break and had nothing better to do, he joined them.

"Well, this is a nice surprise," said Abby as she hugged Austin.

"I even brought a gift for the hostess." He opened his jacket and lifted a small plastic soda bottle filled with *coquito* from his inside pocket.

"Yummy! Keep it hidden until we're downstairs."

Emily slapped Austin's arm and said, "Are you insane? Didn't you hear what Pop said on Christmas Eve?"

"He said I better not *get caught* doing anything stupid. He didn't say not to do stupid things."

"Nice! Your brother is officially in the Social Ninja Club!"

Emily rolled her eyes.

"*Cálmate*, Em. Pop's bark is worse than his bite. You take his threats way too seriously."

"Oh really, well I still have the teeth marks from when he forced me to do community service last June."

Austin laughed. "So you had to read a script about not drinking to the six idiots who showed up drunk at the senior prom. So what? You are *muy sensitiva*, Sis. Laugh it off."

"Whatever," she said. "Easy for you to say since you're away at college."

"You two can fight later," said Abby. She wrapped her hand around Austin's bicep. "Come say *hola* to my parents and then we'll go downstairs. Sarah and Kevin are already here."

After eating and draining the *coquito* bottle, the girls exchanged presents. Abby gave each of them a Coach wristlet, and Sarah bought MAC makeup bags filled with goodies that she said were the perfect colors for the season. Emily gave her friends colored picture frames to match each of their bedrooms. One side of the frame held a picture of them when they were younger, while the other side displayed a recent photo of the group.

"Okay, if you're done ooh-ing, ahh-ing, and hugging, I have something for my girl," said Kevin. He led Emily by the hand to another part of the finished basement so they could have some privacy. They sat cross-legged on the floor facing each other with a gift bag between them. Emily reached in, but Kevin stopped her.

"Wait, I want to explain why I didn't buy you something fancy. I mean, I could've bought you jewelry or something like that, but my dads insisted personal was better than expensive. So . . ." he retrieved one gift from the bag. Emily unraveled the red tissue paper to find silk sunflowers.

"They're summer flowers, as you know since they're your favorite, so I had to get fake ones, which I think is okay because this way you can enjoy them year-round."

Emily smiled. "Thank you. They're beautiful."

"There's more," he said. He offered her a second gift wrapped in red tissue paper, note cards with quotes from famous poets. "Because I know you like to read and write. And there's one more," he said and tapped the gift bag.

She peeked inside. "An insulated lunch bag?" she asked, surprised, and quickly added, "I mean, who couldn't use one, right?"

Kevin laughed. "The gift is inside."

"Coconut ice cream!" she yelled with glee, raising the pint in the air.

"Your favorite. See I pay attention," he said with a smirk. "But, if you think these are stupid, I could run to the mall tomorrow and buy you Michael Kors sneakers or something."

"They're perfect. Thank you." Emily leaned in and kissed him. "I have something for you, too."

He shredded the wrapping paper to find a black steel Fossil watch.

"Whoa, this is awesome!" he said. "Is this because I'm always late?"

"Maybe," she said with a grin.

"Well, I'll be Mr. Punctual from now on," he said, fastening the watch on his wrist. "Go ahead; ask me what time it is."

"What time is it?" she asked with a laugh.

"It's 12:15 a.m."

"In London," she chuckled. "You need to reset it."

As she leaned in to help him, he pulled her on top of him. They laughed and kissed; his hands caressed her back and her cascading hair tickled his face.

"Ah-hem!" Abby coughed to get their attention.

Emily slid off Kevin, who said, "Hey, Abby, ask me what time it is."

"It's time for you to get a room."

"No, seriously," he said with a laugh. "Let me check my new fancy watch. It's . . . oh, wait . . . minus five hours . . . 7:19 p.m."

"The Mayans would be impressed, I'm sure," she said and smiled. "Come join the party."

Hours later, the group fell into siesta mode. Abby rested on one couch, her legs across Austin's lap, while he reclined and propped his feet on a nearby table. Sarah sprawled on the floor with a pillow under her head, as she watched *It's a Wonderful Life* again. Kevin lay on his back on the other couch, with Emily by his side.

"Hey, Em," he said quietly. "Tommy and Elizabeth are taking her sister cosmic bowling. You know, with the black lights and music. Want to go?"

"Sure."

"Should we invite this crew?" he asked while stroking her hair.

"No. I can hang out with you alone, with you and them, or with you and Tommy and Elizabeth, but we all can't hang out together."

"Why not?" he asked with a laugh.

"Trust me. It wouldn't work. Abby would start yapping about paying attention to the little people . . ."

"Like midgets?"

"No," Emily said and laughed.

Abby glanced at the couple and said, "You two are so cute. You have me to thank for this, you know that, right?"

"What's she talking about?" asked Emily.

"Nothing. She's drunk and talking nonsense," he said. "Yep, thanks for having us over, Abby. You're the best. Sleep it off."

Emily giggled and said, "Hey, Kev, will you break up with me if my dad sends me to a Catholic boarding school?"

"Of course not, especially if you have to wear one of those cute uniforms. Totally hot."

She laughed and wiped her eyes.

"Are you crying?" he asked.

"Not really. I'm just so tired and the *coquito* made it worse. I think I'm passing out."

"Go ahead and pass out, Em. I've got you," he said and held her tighter. He kissed her on the head and added, *"Feliz Navidad, mi amor.* I've been practicing. Not bad, right?"

"Yeah, not bad. Merry Christmas," she whispered. She snuggled into him and fell into a deep sleep.

CHAPTER 27

"I hide myself within my flower"

On the way to cosmic bowling, Elizabeth sat in the backseat with Lily. She said they needed to strategize, but really she didn't want to hear it from her mom the whole ride about how she was still grounded and this outing was an exception for Lily and she had to be a responsible older sister. Like she'd ever let something bad happen to Lily.

"I wasn't going to say anything, but I think you have a right to know," said Elizabeth.

Lily widened her eyes. "What is it?"

Their mom's eyes flicked from the road to the backseat through the rearview mirror, clearly nervous about what Elizabeth might say.

"Tommy said it should be boys against girls. I reminded him that they'd be outnumbered since there are three of us and two of them, and his exact words were, 'Well, with Lily, it's more like two and a half, plus I think you girls need all the help you can get.'"

"Oh, no he didn't," said Lily.

"Yes, he did."

"He doesn't know who he's messing with," Lily added and circled her wrists.

"You got that right, sister," Elizabeth said, joining her in the wrist warm-ups.

A smile was evident in their mom's eyes as she glanced at them through the rearview. "Okay, have fun, you two," she said after pulling up to the bowling alley's entrance. "Text me when you want me to pick you up. Not too late."

"Does that mean I get my phone back?" Elizabeth asked, her hands pressed together as if she were begging.

"Nope. You can use Lily's phone."

"Sure, the eleven-year-old has a phone."

"The eleven-year-old didn't swear at a teacher and go three rounds with a row of lockers," said Lily.

"Good point," said Elizabeth.

As Lily hopped out of the car, she called behind her, "Later, Julia."

Elizabeth shrugged, while her mom gave her a look that could only mean "I wonder how she learned that."

Tommy spotted the girls soon after they pushed through the main entrance doors and peeled off their winter coats.

"What the . . . ?" Tommy nudged Kevin in the arm and pointed. The girls walked side by side, wearing jeans and matching black shirts trimmed in cobalt blue. Both wore their hair in two French braids and carried their own bowling balls in matching blue-and-black bags.

"Are you serious?" asked Kevin.

Elizabeth answered by pulling out her own shoes, a resin sack, towel, and tape.

"Aw, man," he said. "We're screwed."

"I think Emily should be on our team," said Tommy.

"Oh, no," said Lily. "You want to make sexist comments? Now, you have to deal with the consequences." She laced her fingers and flipped them over, cracking her knuckles.

Elizabeth stood beside her. She tilted her head from side to side, a loud pop generated with each movement. "Emily bowls with us and we need a few minutes to warm up."

"Warm up?" Kevin threw up his hands and turned to Tommy. "Dude, we're dead."

Emily hesitated and then moved closer to Elizabeth and Lily to change her shoes. While she waited for the Davis girls to finish stretching, her phone buzzed with a text.

Abby: Hey, Em, whatcha doing?

Emily: Bowling.

Abby: Really? w/Kevin?

Emily: Yes & Tommy, Elizabeth, & her little sister.

Abby: Oh . . . never mind.

Emily: What?

Abby: Sarah & I are going to the movies. We were going to invite you, but you're busy.

Emily: You could meet us here.

Abby: Ummm . . . no, thanks.

Emily: Maybe I can meet up with you later.

Abby: Don't worry about it.

"Hey, Em, you ready? You're up first," said Kevin.

"Oh, sorry," she mumbled as she tucked her phone into her pocket. She held her sweaty hands over the dryer for a few seconds.

"Check her out, trying to act all professional like her partners," Tommy joked.

Emily wiped her hands on her jeans and bowled twice without finesse. Two pins toppled. "Sorry," she said again.

"Shake it off, Delgado. We got this," said Elizabeth as she rubbed her sister's shoulders.

Emily grinned and returned to her seat. Kevin sat sideways on the plastic chairs, one leg stretched out, the other on the ground. Emily fit herself into the space in front of him and released the breath she was holding as Kevin wrapped his arms around her. He pecked her on the neck and squeezed her tight. She sank into him.

Lily's ball crashed into the pins. Strike! Elizabeth hooted and taunted Tommy, who rubbed a hand over his recent buzz cut as if that would bring him luck. While Tommy bowled, Elizabeth toweled off her ball and handled her resin sack.

"Those two need to kiss and get it over with," Kevin said to Emily. "Watch this." He cleared his throat and raised his voice, "So, this is kind of like our first double date, right?"

Elizabeth launched the resin sack in Kevin's direction.

Emily ducked as the pack sailed toward them and hit Kevin in the eye.

"Don't worry, Delgado, I've got good aim," said Elizabeth.

"That's all you have to say? How about an apology, Davis?" asked Kevin, laughing and blinking back tears as he lobbed the sack to her. "You know, be a good role model to your sister."

Elizabeth rolled her eyes, but realized Lily was watching and laughing like everyone else. She winked at Lily and added, "Sorry, Kevin, it slipped out of my hand."

The group grooved and played as dance music blared and anything white glowed fluorescent under the black lights. Tommy shook his head at Elizabeth as they rested between games.

"What?"

"You surprise me," he said. "How did I not know you were like a semi-pro bowler?"

Elizabeth chuckled. "We were in a league with my dad, but I kept quiet about it when we moved here and I realized most of the girls in town were semi-pro jazz dancers." She flashed a smile and shook her hands.

"Yeah, you and jazz hands don't go together," Tommy said with a laugh. "Like you cared what the jazz girls thought."

"I did," she said and looked down. "Not anymore. Whatever. The bottom line is I have dark secrets lurking beneath the surface." She snarled in her creepy-horror-chick way. "You don't know everything about me, Tomás."

"I'd like to," he said.

Elizabeth's eyes widened and her heart raced as Tommy's warm, brown eyes drank in every inch of her face.

"Oh," was all she managed to say.

Tommy laughed and rubbed his head. "You've got a way with words, Davis, you know that? Which reminds me, I wanted to ask the committee a question."

"What committee? What question?"

Tommy stood and faced the others.

"You may not know this, but Davis writes all of this amazing stuff in her journal."

"How do you know it's amazing?" she asked.

"I have the floor, Miss Davis. Please don't interrupt."

Elizabeth covered her face with her hands as Tommy continued, "I'm sure it's awesome because you're smart and creative and deserve to be immortalized like that chick in the Shakespeare sonnet we read in class. I want to publish one of her poems in the newspaper. What does the committee think?"

Elizabeth protested, "When did this become a group decision?"

But everyone else shouted over her, "Yes! Do it!"

Lily bounced to Elizabeth's side. "That would be awesome! You'd be a published author! And I'd be the sister of a famous poet!"

"Not exactly, Lily. Did you miss the part about it being published in the *school newspaper*?"

"Hey . . ." said Tommy.

"Sorry, but it'd be no big deal," said Elizabeth.

As soon as the words were out of Elizabeth's mouth,

Kevin punched her in the arm and yelled, "Gotcha! If I can't say it, you can't, either."

In response, Lily wound up and punched him in the groin.

"Don't hit my sister!" she yelled as Kevin doubled over.

"Lily! You shouldn't hit people." Elizabeth firmly held her sister's shoulders to seem stern but ended up laughing so hard, she was wheezing. Emily alternated between laughing and acting the part of the sympathetic girlfriend.

Once Elizabeth regained control, she sat and pulled Lily close.

"Seriously, Lily, don't hit people. We can dye your hair purple next year or something, but don't act like me that way, okay?" Elizabeth's breath caught in her throat. She swallowed hard and added, "Thanks for having my back, but it's not your style, Lillian Grace."

"It was only Kevin and it was pretty funny," Lily said with a smile.

"True, but no more, okay?"

"Okay," said Lily and they sealed the deal with a fist-bump.

"Now, let's kick their asses the right way," said Elizabeth. "You're up."

Lily tilted her head from side to side like Elizabeth, but nothing cracked. She grabbed her bowling ball and let it fly. Crash! Another strike.

After their last game, Kevin grouped the others together and snapped a picture. Everyone, except Elizabeth, contorted their faces into silly poses. She flashed her "jazz smile" and held up her middle finger.

As they zipped up coats and dug out mittens and scarves, Lily shouted, "Snow!" and sprinted through the main doors; the others followed close behind. Large flakes danced with the whirling wind and landed on readied tongues and lifted faces.

"Come on, we still have time before Mom gets here," said Lily. She led the pack across the street and up the block to the elementary school yard.

Tommy and Kevin scooped up snow and packed it, but the fluffy flakes prevented them from having a real snowball fight. Lily twirled and flopped backward into a pile. Emily and Elizabeth joined her, their arms spread wide and flapping to create their angels' wings.

After, Elizabeth attempted a sneak attack on Tommy, but he spotted her coming and dodged her tackle. She landed face-first in the snow, rolled over, and laughed. Tommy grabbed her hand and pulled her to her feet.

"So, what do you think about what Kevin said in there about this maybe being our first double date?"

Elizabeth's smile vanished and she shook her head. "Don't do this," she said and bolted.

"Hey, wait!"

Elizabeth stopped and Tommy jogged the few feet to catch up.

Tommy cupped her face and then slid a hand to the back of her neck and pulled her toward him. They wrapped their arms around each other. He whispered, "I'm not like your father. I'd never cheat on you, Elizabeth."

"I want to believe you, but I can't . . ." She stepped back. Tommy buried his hands in his jacket pockets.

"You really don't trust me?"

"I trust you more than I trust myself," she said. "I'm a mess. I mean, I beat up my dad, my mom hates me, and I'm the worst big sister ever. I can't promise you pink paper hearts scattered in your locker and love notes covered in smiley faces."

"Lucky for you, I'm not a fan of pink hearts or smiley faces," he said with a grin. "All I want is you, Elizabeth. Your family drama can't last forever and when that gets better, so will you."

Elizabeth shook her head. "Maybe, but I can't do this right now," she said.

"Will you ever be able to do this?"

Elizabeth stared at the snow beneath her and shifted from one foot to the other. "I don't know," she whispered.

Tommy tilted his head back and closed his eyes. After a while, he swiped a gloved hand down his face, flicked off the water left by the fat melted flakes, and said, "So, I think I'm going to need some space from you, okay?"

"Yeah? How long?"

"I don't know."

"Well, I'm grounded indefinitely, so I guess we'll see after that?"

"I guess," he said.

A car horn pierced the tension between them.

"That's your mom. See ya, slugger," Tommy said and jogged over to Kevin and Emily.

In the car, Elizabeth yanked off her coat, overwhelmed by the heat. At home, she slumped to her bedroom floor, her back against the door, and waited for the quiet that meant everyone was asleep.

She tapped out an e-mail to Tommy on her tablet and stared at it for a few minutes. Instead of pressing "send," she hit "cancel." She crawled into her bed and buried her face into her pillow to stifle her tears and screams.

In another part of town, Emily found Mamá awake in the family room, watching a biography about Marilyn Monroe.

"You didn't have to wait up," Emily said as she plopped down on the sofa.

"I couldn't sleep."

Emily nodded. "I read somewhere that watching TV is the worst thing you can do if you're trying to fall asleep."

"Really?" Mamá flipped through the channels but returned to the Monroe biography. "So, did you have fun tonight?"

"Yeah."

"Nothing crazy, right?"

"No."

"Good." Mamá sat up straighter and winced.

"What's wrong?" asked Emily.

"I have a pain in my neck," she said and rubbed the spot.

"Is it named Edwin Delgado?"

Mamá playfully slapped Emily on the arm and said, "*Cállate.*"

They sat quiet for a long time, mesmerized by the black-and-white images of a young, beautiful Norma Jean. Emily studied her mom as she gazed at the screen, her eyelids heavy but refusing to rest.

"Mamá?"

"*¿Qué?*" she asked, but her gaze remained focused on the television.

"Nothing. Forget it. *Me voy a dormir.*" Emily kissed her mom on the cheek and headed to her room, where she slid into bed and hugged her pillow tight.

An hour later she was still awake, so she turned her phone on to see who was online. As soon as it powered up, her cell buzzed out of control. Kevin had posted the picture of them at the bowling alley. A long list of sarcastic comments followed about the lameness of bowling, the super lameness of hanging out with a sixth-grader, and worst of all, spending time with Elizagoth. Kevin responded to each one in his jokey way. She stayed out of it.

If Emily admitted that she had fun, her friends would bug her even more about pulling away. And if she posted a snarky comment about Tommy and Elizabeth, they probably wouldn't want to hang out with her again. *Who am I kidding?* Emily thought. *They probably didn't even want to hang out with me tonight.* Tommy and Elizabeth are Kevin's friends. They probably invited her only because she's dating Kevin. It's like they had to.

She silenced her phone and turned on the television. A&E had moved on to a biography about Nelson Mandela. Mamá was either asleep on the couch or watching the same show downstairs. Emily hugged her pillow tighter, her eyelids heavy but her mind refusing to rest.

CHAPTER 28

"The Soul has
Bandaged moments –"

JANUARY

On the first day back to school after the holiday break, Elizabeth shuffled into first period and slumped into her assigned seat. She eavesdropped as students around her bragged about their fun-filled vacations. A daydream flashed in her mind of her stuffing dirty socks down their throats. She grinned and felt a little guilty because, aside from the Tommy fiasco, her time off wasn't horrible.

Nana brought her mouth-watering, homemade apple pie, and her mom made an effort at having a normal Christmas dinner, complete with a turkey roasted in their own oven. Last year, they noshed on two store-cooked rotisserie chickens.

Still, holidays would be different from now on. Everyone knew this, but they didn't want to acknowledge it, really.

Instead, they tiptoed around the empty spaces once filled by her father. They clung to the sides of the canyon for fear of falling into the enormous hole that lay inches from where they stood. Every now and then someone mentioned him, and Elizabeth briefly lost her footing. Each time, she needed to reposition herself to maintain stability.

And, of course, there *was* the Tommy fiasco. She glanced at Tommy in class to find Abby stroking a spot on the back of his near-shaved head with her index finger. Elizabeth hunched over her notebook and dragged her pencil across the page repeatedly in a diagonal line. When the page was covered with black, she turned to a new one and started again.

Next to her, Emily sat straight up with her legs crossed under the desk, as usual, but her dark, auburn-tinted hair rested at the base of her neck in a ponytail. Strands dangled in the front, out of the hair tie's grasp. She didn't circle the pieces around her ears like she usually did. She stared at the top of her desk while her palm covered her mouth and her fingers clutched her cheek.

Elizabeth was tempted to ask what her problem was, but if she said something stupid like, *My fish died* or *My friends are mad because I forgot to call them one night*, she'd have to shove a dirty sock down her throat, too.

The minutes passed in slow motion, with Ms. Diaz's voice distorting into nonsense, like the whiny, never-seen teacher in the Charlie Brown cartoons.

"Blah blah blah . . . Tommy wants to make an announcement about the newspaper . . .

"Blah blah blah . . . No, Kevin, it's too cold to have class outside. In the spring, we'll go deep into the nearby woods to write poetry. It's beautiful there, very peaceful . . .

"Blah blah blah . . . Have a great rest of the day. See you tomorrow."

Dazed students snapped back to attention with her final words and the clanging bell. Emily sat still as people around her packed up their belongings and moved toward the door. She peered at Abby and Sarah, who giggled and whispered as they walked out of the room. The girls didn't wait for Emily, who stayed in her seat as the room emptied.

Next to her, Elizabeth ripped pages out of her notebook. Mindless shading covered most of the sheets, but some had poetic phrases she'd jail in a new maximum-security shoe box. Maybe she'd leave this box in her bottom dresser drawer. Lily would discover it after her death. She would have left orders to burn everything, but her sister wouldn't follow through. Her work would be published and the world would realize she was a genius. Those who didn't bother to get to know her when she was alive would read her work and try to figure her out, but it would all be literary guesswork, really.

Elizabeth glanced at the looming black-and-white posters on the nearby wall and laughed at this idea of herself as a modern-day Emily Dickinson. She shoved her papers into her messenger bag and flew out of the room in a few swift steps. A sheet escaped from the crumbled bundle shoved into her bag. Ripped and wrinkled, the freed page fluttered to the floor like an injured bird.

Emily scooped up the paper and opened her mouth to call out to Elizabeth, but her voice failed her and the quick-moving girl was gone. Emily flattened the piece of paper. Her eyes widened as she read it. After, she carefully folded the paper in quarters, smoothing out as many wrinkles as she could. She saw Tommy near the doorway, about to leave.

"Tommy," she called. He didn't hear her. She grabbed her backpack and hustled toward the door.

"Tommy," she said, louder.

He turned. "Yeah?"

"This is Elizabeth's," she said, holding the piece of paper in front of her, flat on her palm, like she was serving it on a tray. "She dropped it. I know you're kind of fighting right now, but I thought maybe you could give it back to her."

Tommy seized the paper from Emily, gave it a fleeting look, and shoved it into his front jeans pocket. He turned and walked out the door, failing to notice the pained expression on Emily's face.

Three weeks later, Abby and Sarah found Emily in the library.

"Hey, girlie-girl, here you are," Sarah chirped.

"Surprise, surprise," added Abby.

Sarah shot Abby a hard look as they sat across from Emily. She smiled wide and said, "So, hot senior Michael Stango is having a party next weekend. You in?"

"I don't know," said Emily. "I told you my dad's running

for the state legislature and I'm pretty much dead if I do anything wrong."

Abby crossed her arms.

"Well, then we could hang out at the mall or go to a movie or something," said Sarah. "We could have a sleepover and do facials. I know it's hard to believe, but this," she framed her face, "doesn't happen on its own."

Emily giggled.

"We miss you, Em," said Sarah. "I know we see each other in school and we hung out a little over the break, but our fabulous, fearless threesome has devolved into a bitchy twosome."

"Hey!" Abby said with a smile. "I prefer to call it being straightforward."

Abby uncrossed her arms and leaned into the table. "Yeah, Em, come out with us. It'll be fun. Plus, like Sarah's face, a social life doesn't just happen. You have to work at it."

They laughed.

"I mean, we know you have Kevin, and you were always on the quiet side, but you've been distant for a while now and we feel shut out," said Sarah. She quickly added, "No offense."

Emily sighed and said, "I know."

"You know?" said Abby. "If you agree with us, do something about it."

"Like what?" asked Emily.

"Snap out of it or take a pill or something and come out with us once in a while."

Emily shook her head. "The thing is, my dad's running for the state legislature."

"We know. So what?" said Abby.

Emily hesitated and glanced at her watch. "I'm late," she whispered. "I can't be late."

"What? Seriously, Em? We're talking about our friendship here and you're worried about your dad and getting to class on time? What is he going to do, make you write a ten-page paper on the importance of punctuality?" Abby stood and grabbed her bag. "If you want to hang out with us, let us know."

Sarah stayed quiet, inspecting Emily's face like a seasoned detective, sniffing out the clues and realizing Emily wasn't talking about her next class.

"Come on, Sarah," Abby called over her shoulder.

Sarah squeezed Emily's hand and said, "We'll talk later, okay?"

Emily nodded. Instead of packing up for class, she stared at the library's large, glass doors closing behind her friends. As she relaxed her gaze, the panes' sharp edges faded and the overhead lights illuminated the dirt and imperfections. Her eyes watered since they were held wide open for so long. A hard blink pushed the tears out, but she wiped them away with the bottoms of her sleeves before anyone noticed.

The next day after school, Emily perched herself on the edge of Sarah's bed as they waited for the pregnancy test results.

"It only takes a few minutes," Sarah said from the doorway of her bathroom.

Emily nodded. "I don't want to check yet. Stay here with me."

"Okay." Sarah sat next to Emily. "So, how late are you?"

"I don't know. Maybe a week."

Sarah rubbed and patted Emily's back. "Have you used protection every time?" she asked.

"Yes."

"But you still think you might be pregnant?" Sarah asked, cocking her head.

Emily shrugged her shoulders. "I'm late. At least I think I am. I don't know. I guess I don't keep track of it very well and the days seem to blend together. I think I should have gotten it by now."

Sarah sighed. "Have you told Kevin?"

"No. I don't want to say anything if it's all in my head."

"If I were a betting girl, I'd put my money on negative. Sometimes my period is off when I'm stressed or I'm exercising too much," said Sarah. "Or you could be overly anxious and thinking the worst because you've got really bad PMS this month. When I get PMS, I think the world is ending in a different way every half hour. I'm a hot mess."

Emily laughed. "You're never a hot mess."

"I told you. This all takes work."

"But, what if I am, Sarah?" A few tears slid down her face.

"Relax. You could be ruining your makeup for nothing. Let's check."

"Wait another minute," said Emily. "Abby's really pissed at me, huh?"

"I think she's more hurt than mad. She doesn't know how to say it, but she misses you, too," said Sarah. "And she's always been like the line-leader, you know? She always has to be president of the club and captain of the team. And then you were the first one to have a real boyfriend. I mean, she's happy for you—she really is—but she's probably a little jealous, too."

"So, she doesn't hate me?" asked Emily.

"No, and I'm sure she'll understand when she has a boyfriend, which could be soooon," sang Sarah.

"Really? Is she dating someone?"

"They're talking, but I've been sworn to secrecy for now," said Sarah. "Time to check, Em."

Emily stared at the carpet while Sarah moved into the bathroom. When she returned to the doorway, she smiled and announced, "It's negative."

Emily flopped back on the bed, her arms thrown above her head.

Sarah joined her on the bed, lying on her side. "I knew it. You were worried for nothing."

"Overreacting as usual, I guess. At least that's what Austin would say. I don't know. I guess now that I think about it, the chances were slim. It's not like that's all we do, and when we do, we're careful. I don't know why I got the idea in my head, but once it was there, I couldn't get rid of it."

"Are you relieved?"

"Yes, I'm definitely relieved." Emily placed a hand on her stomach. "But I feel empty, too. Is that weird?"

"No, that means you're hungry and not because you're pregnant. Come on, let's raid the fridge." Sarah rolled off the bed and pranced out the door. Emily followed her, sauntering downstairs with one hand absentmindedly resting on her belly.

CHAPTER 29

"A poor – torn heart – a tattered heart –"

FEBRUARY 28–MARCH 1

A car rumbled in Emily's driveway on a Saturday afternoon. She pried herself off her bed and shuffled to the window in time to see Abby's brother dropping her off in the driveway. Emily's heart surged. Weeks had passed since Abby declared she was done trying and Emily needed to work at saving their friendship. Emily had initiated small talk at school and alternated where she sat at lunch, but it wasn't enough.

They no longer swung side by side, holding hands to maintain a rhythm. They were out of sync and almost entirely disconnected, which was almost impossible to fix without serious effort. But, Abby was here, in her driveway, unannounced. *I can't believe she's here.*

Emily was about to run downstairs when Austin walked

out of the house. He marched straight to Abby, bent down, and kissed her on the mouth.

The blood drained from Emily's face. She rested her forehead against the chilled window pane and gripped the sill. Abby slid into Austin's car and they drove away.

Hours later, Emily noted the sounds of Austin's return: the car's engine going dead, the slamming of doors, footsteps striding down the hallway. When Austin shut his bedroom door, Emily sprang out of bed and called Abby.

"How long have you been dating Austin?"

"Hey, Em. So nice of you to call me after all this time," she said. "Well, we've been texting for a while and decided to get together since he'd be home this weekend."

"Why didn't you tell me?"

"Because we haven't been talking much."

"I know, but he's my brother."

"Even more reason not to tell you right away. You'd probably think it was gross or he's too old for me or whatever, so I didn't want to say anything unless we were serious."

"Are you serious?"

"Not yet, but I like him a lot."

Emily wanted to be happy for them, but a pit lay in her stomach. One of her best friends came to her home and ignored her, like she was the slightest in the house.

"You didn't even come inside to say 'hi' to me," said Emily.

"You didn't come out to say 'hi' to me. You could've opened your window or waved or something."

"I know."

Abby sighed. "Em, what did you want me to do, invite you on our date? That would've been awkward, don't you think? And even if I did ask you to hang out with us, you would have said no, as usual."

"That's not fair," Emily whispered.

"Really, Em? How many times have you blown us off? You have a boyfriend, fine, but sometimes you say no and stay home, doing *nothing*. And how many times have Sarah and I asked you what's wrong?"

"Oh sure, you told me to down some energy drinks or take a pill and snap out of it. Very sympathetic. Thanks."

"Yes, I'm blunt, but that's nothing new, and that's not the problem here. *You're* the one who disappears into the library and makes excuses when we invite you out. *You* haven't called me in weeks. You didn't even tell me about what happened at Sarah's house. Yeah, she told me, but *you* didn't. *You've* been acting like *I* don't matter, but *I'm* the one who's doing everything wrong? Give me a break, Em."

Abby stopped to catch her breath. Emily stayed quiet.

"You don't know how many times Sarah and I talk about you, trying to figure this out," said Abby. "What did we do? Or did something horrible happen and you're afraid to tell us?"

Emily cried into the phone. "It's not you. Nothing horrible has happened to me."

"Then, what is it?"

"I don't know."

"What do you mean? You're the only one who can know."

"I don't know, everything's all messed up, and maybe it's

all my fault, but when I saw you today, I thought everything was going to be okay, but you weren't here for me."

"Okay, now you sound like you're jealous or something."

"Of course, I'm jealous. We were in a relationship first. We've been best friends since kindergarten and you come to my house and don't even say hello. You want to hang out with my brother instead of me. Yeah, I'm jealous. Why wouldn't I be?"

"So, let me get this straight, you're *jealous* that I'm dating your brother?"

"Yeah, and I guess what I'm really saying is I don't want you dating my brother."

"You can't tell me what to do, Em."

"But you can tell me and everyone else what to do?"

"I never tell you what to do. I tell you how it is. There's a difference," said Abby. "You know what? I'm tired of being blamed for everything. I'm done."

Minutes after Abby hung up, she posted a vague yet attention-getting comment about "that awkward moment when one of your best friends professes her love for you."

"Aw, does this mean you and Emily kissed and made up? I hate it when my girls are fighting," wrote Sarah. "Love you both!"

"Um, no, like I mean she *really* professed her love for me, I think. It was weird. I'll text you."

A string of comments followed, but the one that caught Emily's attention most was from Olivia, who sits in Emily's seat when she has lunch with Kevin. She wrote, "I guess getting

Kevin to hook up with her was a waste of time. Maybe Sue Huntington, that tomboy freshman, is more her type."

Getting Kevin to hook up with me? A wave of nausea rippled through Emily's body. She rushed to the bathroom and heaved into the toilet, but nothing came up. She sank to the floor and pressed her face on the cold tiles until her stomach unclenched and her body felt cool all over.

But another thought forced her into the fetal position: on Monday, Luís the tech-geek-spy would see all the posts, which means so would her dad. And then she'd have to explain what was true, and what wasn't, and she really didn't want to talk to Pop about *any* of it. And no matter what she said, she'd probably be shipped off to a boarding school. She buried her face in her hands and rocked from side to side until she could breathe normally.

After peeling herself off the floor, she gawked at the computer. Kevin had joined the conversation, posting comments in her defense. She considered posting something, but didn't have the energy. Her phone buzzed constantly as Kevin texted and called her. *Tomorrow*, she thought as she shut down the computer and turned off her cell phone. *Tomorrow, I'll talk to Kevin. He has some explaining to do.*

The next morning, Emily's family went to church without her, leaving her to deal with her "painful cramps." When they left, she texted Kevin to come over. She raced around the bedroom, shoving clothes into drawers or tossing them into the hamper. Anything else was piled into corners, chucked into the closet, or shoved under the bed. That done, she turned to getting herself ready.

When the doorbell rang, she lifted her bedroom window and yelled down to him that the front door was open, but to close and lock it behind him. She stood in the middle of her room and waited. Her pulse raced. She breathed deeply a few times before he entered through the door. He walked straight to her, reaching out to hug her, but she pulled away.

"Em . . . ," he started.

She cut him off. "I need to ask you something, and I want the truth."

"Okay," he said.

"Promise?"

"Promise. Scout's honor," he said, raising three fingers.

"You were a Boy Scout?" She was skeptical.

"No, I can't support anything that doesn't support my dads. I had to learn how to start fires on my own," he said and grinned.

"This isn't a joke," she responded.

"I'm serious, but fine, I get it. I just wanted to make you smile a little . . ."

"Was our first kiss a setup?" Emily blurted.

He stood quiet for a while and then said, "I just promised not to lie to you, so I won't."

Emily shook her head. She thought she wanted to hear it, but now she wanted to cover her ears. *No. Please, no.* She almost begged him to lie to her, but he opened his mouth and said, "Yes."

She crossed her arms and forced herself to remain upright.

"Was this summer a setup, too?" She wrapped her arms around her middle and buried her fingertips into her sides.

"No."

"I don't believe you," Emily said. She sat on the bed, pressed her palms into the mattress, and shut her eyes. Kevin kneeled in front of her, resting his hands on either side of her.

"I'm not lying," he said. "Don't be mad, Em, please. I wouldn't have kissed you if I didn't like you. That's the truth. So, yeah, Abby said you liked me, and she encouraged me to do it, but it's not like she forced me. I wanted to, just like I wanted to see you over the summer. After you dropped me and all, I probably wouldn't have even tried again if Abby didn't suggest it before she left for Italy."

"She what?" Emily said, snapping her head up.

"Yeah, she was like, 'Hey, you should text Em if you're bored.' "

Emily pushed him away. "Is that why you texted me? Because you had nothing better to do?"

"No, that came out wrong. It was like a friendly nudge in your direction. It wasn't all Machiavellian. Nice one, right? See, I'm not *always* daydreaming about you in class."

Emily shook her head and closed her eyes again.

"Sorry. Not funny," Kevin said and then inched his way

onto the bed next to her. "She wanted us to get together, don't you see? It was just like the notes she used to pass people in elementary school that said, 'Do you like so-and-so? Check one' and then there were three boxes with 'yes,' 'no,' and 'maybe,' and then she'd set up a play date at recess."

Emily opened her eyes and smiled slightly at the memory.

"She wasn't trying to be sneaky in a bad way and hurt you. And, you know what? I'm glad she played matchmaker with us." He reached for her hand. She let him and shifted her body toward him.

"I thought this one thing was mine—ours—that this was about us, not about her or anyone else," she said.

"It has been all about us," said Kevin, turning his body to face her. "I kept my promise. I never posted anything about us until last night, when everything exploded. But I had to say something because I knew you wouldn't. Before that, though, I never talked to anyone about our relationship, except for Tommy, Elizabeth, and my parents, but they don't really count, do they? I know I'm rambling and you probably hate me, but I need you to know that I think we're great together, Em. You mean everything to me."

Emily's eyes softened and she squeezed Kevin's hand. He leaned in and planted a kiss near her ear. He brushed his cheek against hers and then made a trail of small, gentle kisses to her lips. Her body relaxed and tingled all over, the same way it did when they first kissed. She wrapped her arms around his neck and kissed him. But, Emily couldn't focus on the moment, his lips tenderly touching hers, his hands soft and warm on her waist. This time, the outside world didn't fade away.

Emily pulled back and started to cry.

"What's wrong? Why are you crying?"

She shook her head and said, "You need to go. My parents and brother will be home soon."

"I don't want to leave you this way."

"I'll be fine," she lied. "You can't be here when they get home. My dad would kill me for sure."

Before he left, he held her tight and said, "Everything's going to be okay, Em."

She stared at Kevin through her tear-blurred vision. Abby had orchestrated everything, nudging him and pushing her. They were fools, moving predictably with each tug of their strings. And last night's online scrape was only the beginning. Emily would have to face everyone at school, and her dad would know soon, which would trigger another onslaught. *Everything's going to be okay?*

"I don't know, Kev," she said and shook her head. "I can't think straight and my family will be home soon. You really have to leave."

She kissed him hard and then let him go.

Minutes after he left, she deleted all of her social media accounts and blocked several numbers on her cell phone, including Kevin's.

When prompted electronically, *"Are you sure?"* she hesitated before hitting "Yes."

CHAPTER 30

"Alone and in a Circumstance"

MARCH 2

Emily waited in her bedroom, with her coat on but unzipped, and her backpack hanging on her shoulders. She stared at the second hand circling her watch's face. Her plan was to sprint downstairs and out the front door with enough time to make it to the bus stop and zero time to chitchat with her family in the kitchen.

Austin intercepted Emily as she bounded down the stairs.

"I'll drive you to school today," he said. He also wore his coat, ready to go.

"Okay," she said, relieved because a ride meant she'd dodge Sarah and Abby on the bus.

As soon as they were on the road, Austin said, "I'm sorry about what happened."

Emily nodded.

"I talked to Abby and told her to back off. I hope that helps."
Emily nodded again but didn't respond.

"It's stupid high school shit, Em. Don't worry about it."

"You're talking about my life, Austin."

"I'm sorry," he said and sighed. "What I mean is you and Abby have been friends forever. Isn't there the slightest chance she'll apologize in a few days and you'll be friends again?"

"Not a chance," said Emily. "It's as likely as Pop saying, 'So, you've had a boyfriend for months, which means you've been lying to me and Mamá every time you've left the house. That's okay, we forgive you. And your classmates think you might be bisexual and in love with your best friend. No problem. My people will somehow fit that into my ultraconservative campaign.'"

"Good point, but guess what? Pop is leaving this morning for some convention. He won't be back until Saturday. The even better news is Luís called in sick with the flu, so he'll be down for a few days. You've got some time, probably until this weekend, before you need to face Pop."

Emily nodded again. "Thanks for the ride," she said when Austin stopped in front of the school's main entrance.

"Hey," he said and grabbed her arm. "I'm going back to Amherst today, but if you need me to intimidate anyone big-brother style, say the word."

"Thanks." Emily pushed in her earbuds and cranked the volume on her iPod before entering school. She strolled half-way to her locker but decided to hide out in the nurse's office for as long as possible. After the last bell rang, signaling the start of classes, Emily ambled to her locker in near-empty hallways. Still, the few people who passed her jabbed her with snide comments. Nicole Taylor whispered, "I'm friends with Sue Huntington. I can set you up, if you want," and Anthony Ramos yelled, "Can I get a videotape of you and Abby together?"

Emily didn't respond. She almost ripped up the note on her locker, but she recognized Kevin's handwriting: *You've disappeared from all electronic forms of communication, so I'm writing a good, old-fashioned note to say hi and I hope you're okay and I'll find you later.*

Emily tossed the note into her locker and camped in the library for the rest of the period, sitting on the floor in the nonfiction section, where no one would find her. English and lunch were the only periods she shared with her friends. Avoiding them at lunch would be easy, but she couldn't cut English every day, and she'd have to see them in the halls and on the bus. Plus, Kevin knew her schedule, so he'd probably wait outside her classes to talk to her. She could blast her iPod to shut out the whispers and crude remarks, but she couldn't elude Kevin or her friends forever.

After the period two bell rang, she walked past her locker and retrieved another note from Kevin: *You skipped English. I know because someone said they spotted you this morning, but you weren't in class. Call me Sherlock. Anyway, cutting class is more Elizabeth's thing, not yours. I'm worried about you. Find me later.*

Emily walked different routes to her classes and arrived a

few minutes late to each one to avoid crowds. Music blared in her ears and she avoided eye contact. In between classes, she received two more notes from Kevin.

I haven't seen you all day. Well, it's only third period, but still, this is unusual. It's like you're purposely avoiding me. Did I do something wrong?

Seriously, Emily, what's going on? Find me or leave me a note.

Emily scribbled on a ripped piece of notebook paper and folded it so the square fit in her palm. Walking down the hall, she purposely bumped her shoulder into Elizabeth's.

"What the . . . ?!" Elizabeth stopped when she saw Emily. They locked gazes and Emily slipped the note into Elizabeth's hand and kept walking.

At lunchtime, Elizabeth met Emily at the clearing.

"It's freezing out here, Delgado. Make it quick."

Emily grinned. "It's not that cold. I thought you were a badass."

"This badass likes to be warm," she said with a smile. "So, I heard about what happened. How are you holding up? Not that I care."

"I'm fine," she said with a smirk.

"Liar."

"Yeah," Emily admitted. "I'm lying. Everything's all screwed up."

"So, Kevin was prodded by Abby, so what? Think of her as the teen version of match.com. Kevin really likes you. Trust me, I have to hear about it all the freakin' time."

"Maybe," said Emily. She zipped her coat to the top and bounced to keep warm. "But I can't be around any of them right now."

"Sounds familiar," Elizabeth said and threw up her hood.

"What's going on with you? Not that I care," Emily said with a smile.

"Tommy and I still aren't talking. We only spoke once last week, but he was all formal, in the role of editor, not friend. He asked me again about publishing one of my poems in the newspaper. I knew he was trying to break the ice, but we're still living in Glacierville."

Emily remembered the poem she gave Tommy in January. "What did you say?"

"I said maybe."

"Your maybe usually means yes."

Elizabeth smiled. "Don't act like you know me, Delgado. They don't call me Enigmatic Elizabeth for nothing."

"No one calls you that," said Emily.

"True," she said.

They laughed and stomped on the melting snow for a few moments.

"So, I know we're not really friends, but can you do me a favor?" asked Emily.

"What?"

"Can you give this to Kevin for me?" She pulled a small envelope from her pocket.

"Oh, you want me to deliver a message for you. That's why I'm here. Got it. No problem."

Before Emily could say anything more, Elizabeth snatched the note, turned on her heel, and flashed the peace sign over her shoulder as she marched back to school. She found Kevin peering through the library's glass doors.

"You can go in, you know. They don't charge you to enter."

"Hey, Davis. I was trying to find Emily, but I didn't want to go in and scour the place and have her think I was stalking her. Plus, I owe them a way-overdue book, so I figured standing out here was my best option."

"Whatever," Elizabeth said and shook her head. "Listen, your girlfriend asked me to give this to you."

"Thanks, Davis," he said, taking the note. He ripped open the envelope and grinned because the card was from the set he gave her at Christmas. Inside, she wrote: *Remember when you said if I wanted or needed you to do something, you would? Well, I need to be alone for a while. Seriously, if you love me, you'll give me some space so that I can figure out what to do. I'm sorry."*

Kevin stood motionless. Not knowing what to say, Elizabeth turned to leave.

"Hey, Davis, I have a message for you, too," said Kevin. "Tommy needs an answer about the poem."

"Fine," she said. "I'll write him a stupid poem, okay?" She stomped a few paces and turned around. "And tell him if he wants to talk to me, he can do it himself." After several more steps, she pivoted again and shouted, "And tell your girlfriend not to use me as her carrier pigeon ever again."

Kevin strolled to Emily's locker and taped a note to the

outside. He kissed his fingertips and pressed them on the paper before walking away: *My dearest Emily, Okay. I'll give you space, but I hope this doesn't mean we're broken up. In my head, we're on a temporary break, like you're on an unexpected vacation and I can't wait for you to get back. Send me a postcard once in a while, okay? I'll miss you.*

Emily's hands shook as she tucked the note into her coat pocket. Of course, he'd respect her wishes. But if that's what she wanted, why did her stomach plummet with that carved-out hollow feeling when she read his response? She rested her head against the locker's chilled metal until the clanging bell jolted her out of her reverie. Instead of going to her last two classes, she walked out a side door into the cold.

CHAPTER 31

"I'm Nobody! Who are you?"

MARCH 6

Elizabeth stuffed in her earbuds and cranked the volume as she got off the bus and entered the school. The music pounded in her head as she navigated the hallways to her locker, shutting out anyone's attempt to wish her a good morning.

More students than usual looked her way and mouthed something to her. Weird. She nodded at them, her way of saying, "Good morning," but she wondered, *Why are so many people trying to talk to me? Did the principal deliver some fuzzy, love-thy-neighbor announcement? Do I have something on my face?*

Elizabeth arrived at her locker and dropped her bag at her feet. She glanced suspiciously at the people around her, as she circled through her combination. Students continued to utter comments to her. She tried to lip-read, but couldn't decipher what they said. One girl placed her hand on her heart and wore an "Awww" expression on her face. Elizabeth opened her locker and shoved her coat inside. She cautiously pulled out the earbuds, nervous about what she'd hear.

The boy with the locker next to hers said, "Cool poem," and slammed his locker shut.

"What?" she asked, her eyes wide.

Instead of repeating himself, he said, "Deep," and walked off.

Elizabeth stuffed the books she needed for her first two classes into her bag, slung the strap over her shoulder, and slammed her locker. She walked swiftly toward her first period English class.

"Good job," someone said.

"Thanks," she said automatically. *Wait. For what?*

She walked faster.

"Great poem," another person said.

"Brava," said another.

She power walked now, her pulse throbbing at her temples. She rounded a corner and bumped into Kevin.

"Whoa," he said. "Slow down there, Shakespeare-ette, or should I say, e.e. davis? Didn't think I knew e.e. cummings was a poet, huh? I'm full of surprises. Shock and awe, baby."

"What are you talking about? Why are you calling me strange names?"

"Your poem was published today," he said matter-of-factly.

"What the hell are you talking about?" she said more forcefully.

"The school newspaper. It came out today. Your poem is in it."

Elizabeth dropped her bag to the floor and grabbed the newspaper from him. She flipped frantically through the pages. "How is that possible? I didn't hand one in."

"He already had one, and you told me the other day it was fine," Kevin said as he picked up her bag. "Page twenty. In the creative writing section." Elizabeth found the page and saw it—the poem she wrote in English class after the holiday break, the one she thought was part of the wad of paper she stuffed into a shoe box later that day.

She holds the wishbone out to me.
Ripped from the turkey's chest,
The blood is gone, the bone is dry.
A plaything in our hands.

I hold my breath and yank my side.
Snap. I lost. She asks me:
So, sister, what did you wish for?
I don't want to hurt her:

A girl who dances through the house
To a tune in her head.
A girl who points out birds and bugs
Like they are new to her.

I wished for a pony, I say.

She laughs, which makes me smile.

So what did you wish for? I ask.

To be complete again.

She looks down at the broken bone,

Clutches it tight and smiles,

As if the pieces weren't cracked,

As if time could rewind.

Elizabeth stood frozen as the blood drained from her face. Her vision blurred and her heartbeat pounded in her ears.

"Are you okay?" Kevin asked.

"No."

Kevin grabbed her arm near the elbow; she clutched his forearm for support.

"You need to breathe," he said. "Breathe deeply. Come on . . . in and out . . . deeply."

Elizabeth inhaled, filling her lungs to the bursting point, and then released the air in a steady stream. As she did this again and again, blood rushed through her body: up her calves and thighs, down her arms, and into her fingertips. Her eyes danced and her hands quivered from the adrenaline coursing through her veins. A million thoughts flooded her mind, and then one needed her immediate attention.

She stood straight and released Kevin's forearm. He dropped his hold, but his hand lingered in case he needed to grab her again. She shoved the paper into Kevin's chest and ran at full speed through the hallway, dodging slow-moving students and ignoring teachers' calls to walk. She flew down a flight of stairs and sprinted through another hallway to reach the journalism classroom.

The room was empty, as expected, since students were selling newspapers throughout the building. She marched to the back of the classroom, where a door led to a former storage area now used as an office. Tommy heard the footsteps and got up to see who it was. He bumped into Elizabeth as she raced through the doorway. He stepped back and laughed.

"Hey, sorry, I didn't see you coming," he said.

Elizabeth pulled back her fist and launched it forward, punching Tommy hard in the stomach.

His body bent forward from the hit, his hand instinctively moving to his stomach. She lifted an open palm, ready to slap him in the face, but he raised an arm and blocked her.

He backed off with both hands in front of him.

"What the hell, Elizabeth? What are you doing?" he asked with a nervous laugh in his voice.

"You had no right! You had no right!" she yelled as she slapped at his hands and arms. "Those are my thoughts and feelings! You had no right to publish it! Who do you think you are?!"

Tommy grabbed her by the wrists to stop her from thrashing him.

"Stop. Elizabeth, stop." He wasn't laughing anymore. He pulled her close to him, still holding her wrists. "Calm down."

After a few moments, her fists unfurled, but her body remained tense. Her breathing came in short bursts, like a bull snorting between attacks.

"Let me go," she ordered through gritted teeth.

Tommy did and raised his hands in the air, like a criminal does when caught. After a second, he dropped his hands to his sides.

They stared at each other.

"Kevin said you agreed," he said.

"I said I'd write one for you. I didn't know you had one."

Tommy sighed and ran his hand over his head.

"How did you get it?" she asked.

"Emily Delgado . . ."

Without hearing another word, Elizabeth ran out of the room and headed back toward her first period class. As she maneuvered around students, the same teachers told her to slow down. She nodded at them and kept running.

Elizabeth spotted Emily's brown hair in the near distance as the girl approached Ms. Diaz's classroom. Elizabeth ran at full speed until she was directly behind Emily. Without breaking her stride, Elizabeth bent her arms at the elbows and then released them into Emily's back. Students gasped and moved out of the way. Emily tumbled to the ground. Her outstretched arms saved her from falling face-first to the floor.

After a few moments, she pushed herself to her knees and placed a foot on the floor. Someone screamed at her, but she couldn't make out the words. Everything seemed to move in slow motion. She wanted to stand up and see who pushed her. She hoped it was an accident, someone running while messing around with a friend.

She turned her body to face the screaming. Elizabeth's face told her this wasn't an accident.

"You had no right!" Elizabeth yelled.

"What?" Emily asked in a low voice. Her hands and knees ached, but she tried to stand. As Emily looked up, Elizabeth's fist came down hard and fast. Emily was back on the floor. She didn't try to get up this time. She propped herself up with her elbow and clutched her cheek with her other hand. Tears filled her eyes and spilled over.

She stared at Elizabeth who was still screaming. Emily could only hear a ringing sound in her ear. Through her tears, she saw other students near them and teachers running toward them. She forced herself to focus, to hear what Elizabeth was yelling.

"Who the fuck do you think you are?"

Emily looked directly at Elizabeth. "I'm nobody," she said evenly.

Elizabeth stopped, her eyes locked on Emily's, her pulse racing. She began to breathe deeper, slower, when Ms. Diaz grabbed her arm right above the elbow.

"Elizabeth . . ." Ms. Diaz's calming voice was near her ear. The tension and anger drained from Elizabeth's body, while sorrow and regret filled her up. Elizabeth shut her eyes as the tears came.

The principal arrived and helped the teachers to disperse the crowd before he turned his attention to Elizabeth. Ms.

Diaz let go of Elizabeth's arm, walked to Emily, and crouched down to help her off the floor.

Elizabeth opened her eyes and looked at Emily, who was still on the ground and staring directly at her. She held Emily's gaze as long as she could before the principal ordered her to turn and walk.

CHAPTER 32

"I am ashamed – I hide –"

In the main office, Emily sat at a small table near the secretaries' desks. She pressed an ice pack to her cheek, a few minutes at a time, for as long as she could stand the cold. Her eyes were puffy from crying, her face splotchy red.

Tommy sat in a chair on the other side of the table. He pushed the chair a few feet away to create some distance between him and Emily. He knew she did nothing wrong, that he alone made the decision to publish the poem. He looked at her with pleading eyes, waiting for a moment to apologize. Emily was uninviting. She either closed her eyes or stared at a spot on the table in front of her.

Tommy peered over his shoulder at Elizabeth, who sat away from her victims at a desk outside the principal's office.

Elizabeth sat sideways so the desktop was to her right.

She was bent at the waist, her feet flat on the floor, her elbows on her knees and her head cradled in her hands. She stared at the ground and rocked back and forth.

"Hey," Tommy called to her.

"No talking, please," a secretary said curtly.

Elizabeth raised her head.

"I'm fine. No damage done. I'm so sorry," he said.

"I said no talking, Mr. Bowles," the secretary said forcefully.

"Sorry," Tommy said. "It won't happen again."

"You are still talking."

Tommy pulled two fingers across his lips, miming that he was "zipping it."

After a few moments, Kevin walked out of the principal's office. He was called in to explain what had happened before the incident.

"You are one crazy girl," he said, pointing at Elizabeth.

"That's enough," said the principal. "Please go back to class."

Kevin stopped at the table and patted Tommy on the back. "Emily, are you okay?" he asked softly. Emily kept her eyes closed, her face pressed against the ice pack. She shook her head, no.

"Good-bye, Mr. Wen-Massey," said the principal, who led Kevin out of the office by the elbow. "You're next, Mr. Bowles."

Tommy stood up and said, "I'm sorry," to Emily, even though she wasn't looking at him and didn't respond.

Elizabeth kept her head in her hands as Tommy walked by her. He gently placed his hand on the top of her head. Warmth ran down Elizabeth's neck. She closed her eyes tighter and stopped rocking. Tommy then went into the principal's office and shut the door behind him.

Soon after, Ms. Diaz entered the office. She knew she couldn't get involved, but she could offer a little support. She lightly squeezed Emily's shoulder. Emily managed the slightest of smiles, but quickly returned to her previous pose.

Ms. Diaz grabbed a chair and sat across from Elizabeth. The whites of her eyes were streaked with red, spiderweb veins.

Elizabeth cleared her throat and said, "What have I done?"

"Tell me what happened."

"She got my poem somehow. He published it." She added in a whisper, "It was about my dad."

Ms. Diaz sighed. "I understand, but . . ."

"I know," said Elizabeth. "What I did was inexcusable. I'm a horrible person. Kevin's right. I'm crazy."

"You're not horrible or crazy. We all make mistakes. Big ones. Grand Canyon-size mistakes."

"Yeah, this is a big one," said Elizabeth. "I deserve whatever I get. I'll be suspended."

"Yes," Ms. Diaz said.

"Will I be expelled?"

"I don't think so."

"Will I be arrested?"

"Maybe."

"My mom is going to kill me." Elizabeth dropped her head into her hands and sobbed.

Unsure of what to say, Ms. Diaz let her cry.

"I'm not even so worried about the punishment part," Elizabeth said. "I mean, I'm not thrilled about being suspended, and I'll be devastated if I'm arrested, but that's not what scares me most."

"What is it, then?"

"I couldn't stop myself, Ms. D. It was like that day with my dad." Elizabeth crossed her arms in front of her stomach and leaned her head against the wall. "I feel sick."

"That's actually a good thing," said Ms. Diaz. "It means you don't want something like this to happen again. Maybe this is the moment when something clicks inside you and things will start to change."

"I don't know . . . I don't hear anything clicking."

Just then, the bell rang.

"Hold on," said Ms. Diaz. She stood and jogged down the short hallway that led to the adjoining guidance offices. Ms. Gilbert's door was closed with a "Do Not Disturb" sign on it. She returned to Elizabeth.

"I have a class, but I'll talk to Ms. Gilbert and the principal," she said. "I'm monitoring Saturday detention. I'll ask the principal if you can start your punishment tomorrow so we can talk some more. Even if he says no, come to the school anyway. Have your mom call me if it's a problem. Promise me you'll come."

Elizabeth nodded and then dropped her head into her hands.

Ms. Diaz walked into the main office and ripped a piece of paper from a pad on the front counter. On it, she wrote:

Suzanne,

Elizabeth is in crisis. You need to talk to her ASAP.

Call me when you can.

—Emilia

Ms. Diaz folded the note and handed it to the secretary.

"Please give this to Ms. Gilbert as soon as possible. It's urgent."

CHAPTER 33

My Letter to the World

Remember when I said my plank in reason broke? That I was falling and would hit the ground at some point? It happened. Of course, it happened. Before yesterday, every part of me ached. After what happened, I was completely numb, like every inch of me was wrapped tight in an Ace bandage.

I read Dickinson's poem "The Soul has Bandaged moments —" and it made me think. A bandage covers a wound and helps it to heal, but it also masks the hurt. And if the broken part of you is bound too long or too tightly, doesn't it make everything worse? At some point, don't you have to rip off the bandage, expose the wound, and deal with the pain? So whether you're injured or healing, it hurts.

I guess numb isn't so bad, then, because I don't want to hurt anymore. I don't want to hurt anyone else, either. I hope you understand now that I cared and tried to fight the monster inside me, but it won. Please don't worry, Ms. Diaz, I'm not afraid. I know it's the right thing to do. As I finish writing this, I feel stronger than I've felt in a long time. I'm ready for what comes next.

CHAPTER 34

"This World is not Conclusion"

MARCH 7

Elizabeth smacks her alarm clock, shutting it off seconds after it screams for her attention. She rolls over and pulls her comforter tight around her. She's exhausted but needs to get up. She doesn't expect sleep to come but hopes for a few more minutes of quiet before she has to face the day.

Her eyes are shut tight, but she can't escape the sights and sounds of the rage, pain, and humiliation that started in school yesterday and followed her home. She wants to stay in bed but this won't help her situation. Her mom will freak out if she wakes up and finds Elizabeth home instead of at Saturday detention.

She must leave the house, but where will she go? She hadn't decided before going to bed: the park, the cemetery, or the woods near the high school? She sits up and pushes herself out of bed to start her morning routine. When she's ready, Elizabeth stops once more in the hallway bathroom. She opens the medicine cabinet, pops open a bottle, and tosses four pills into her mouth. She swallows them easily with a handful of water. She studies herself in the mirror for a second and shakes her head.

"Damn," she says. "I look like shit." She takes the bottle of pills with her.

She leaves the bathroom and pauses at her sister's bedroom door. Lily must be exhausted. She often wakes up early, even on weekends, but last night was a late one for everyone. Mom ordered Lily to bed at some point but was too busy arguing with Elizabeth to know whether Lily obeyed. When Elizabeth stormed out of the living room, she found Lily sitting on the stairs, her hands over her ears and tears in her eyes. Her mom was right behind Elizabeth, so she escorted Lily upstairs.

"I love you. I'm sorry," Elizabeth says softly before heading downstairs.

She leaves a note on the fridge and heads outside with more than enough time to get to the woods. That's where she'll go. She walks unhurriedly and considers which route to take. Her town is eerily quiet. Few cars pass her and she sees only one other person walking in the distance: a girl in jeans, a white coat, and knee-high white boots. Elizabeth doesn't recognize her. She's too far away and her hood is up, hiding her face.

The only students headed to school today are the detention delinquents and the drama geeks who will show up super

early to prepare for the matinee of whatever they're perform-
ing. If this girl is going to school, then she's taking the short-
est route. She must be a drama student. The delinquents are
never eager to attend detention.

Elizabeth checks her watch. She's got plenty of time. She
turns away from the girl walking in the distance and decides
to take the long way.

Ms. Diaz arrives at school with five minutes to spare. After
getting out of the car, she walks to the school's side door
entrance.

Locked.

"Come on," she mutters. As she walks around the perimeter of the school to the front entrance, she says, "It's going to
be one of those days."

Ms. Diaz enters the school and spots a few students in
the lobby, waiting to sign in for Saturday detention. Elizabeth
isn't there like she should be. After yesterday's events, Ms.
Gilbert spoke to Emily and Elizabeth at length. Emily will be
out of school for a few days, and Elizabeth went home after
receiving her punishment.

Ms. Diaz glances at her watch and speed walks to her
classroom to grab a stack of papers to grade during detention. When she walks into the room, she hears the crunching
sound of paper under her boots. A letter was slipped under
the door, along with a larger manila envelope. The last letter
she received was before the holiday break.

She picks them up. "Read First" is written across the front of the letter. "Read Second" is written on the larger envelope. She walks across the room and puts her bag, keys, and the larger envelope on top of her desk. She rips open the first envelope, pulls out the letter, and reads.

3/7

Dear Ms. Diaz,

First, I want to say thanks for letting me write to you and for listening to me this way. I know it may have been weird, but having you as a silent audience has been helpful and comforting at times. I should have written to you more. Maybe it would have helped. But, it's too late for maybes and what-ifs.

On the first day of school, you asked about where we dwell—how we navigate the world. Do you remember that? I told you then I didn't think I was succeeding at figuring things out. Yesterday, everything became clear, and once that happened, I knew exactly what I needed to do.

You said in the spring we'd go deep into the nearby woods to write poetry. I've been there; it's beautiful. I've also been reading Emily Dickinson's poetry and about her life. She has a poem that starts, "This World is not Conclusion." I agree. I believe there's more for us beyond this life, and I hope it's a tranquil, forgiving place.

I need peace, and I'm not willing to wait any longer.

I'll be in the woods. I'm letting you know because I
want to be found sooner rather than later, for my
family's sake. My death will be painful enough for
them. I don't want to be discovered weeks or months
later when I'm a rotting corpse. This way, you'll find
me sleeping, my spirit freed.

Ms. Diaz's shaking hands drop the letter on the floor. She
pivots and runs full speed across the classroom, down a
short maze of hallways, and through a set of double doors
that lead to the grass field. She starts to dart across the field
to the wooded area when she hears her name called.

She turns around and stops in her tracks at once. The
move—coupled with the shock racing through her system—
almost sends her tumbling to the ground. She's stunned to
see Elizabeth nearing the double doors.

Ms. Diaz runs back and grabs Elizabeth by the shoulders.

"What are you doing here?" she demands.

"My punishment starts today," Elizabeth says, shrugging
out of Ms. Diaz's grasp. "I was going to skip it, but then I
remembered that I promised you I'd show up no matter what."

"Where are you coming from?"

"Home. Where else would I be coming from? Well, jail, I
suppose, but they only gave me a ticket, which I think is
technically an arrest, but there were no handcuffs or anything. And I've got the suspension and mandatory counseling
with the school psychologist. No more chitchats with Ms.
Gilbert."

Ms. Diaz stares at the rambling girl and starts to walk backward.

"No. No. No," she says, shaking her head. "Oh my God. It's someone else."

"What? Ms. D, are you okay?"

"No," she says. She shoves her hand inside her vest pocket, walks forward again, and presses her cell phone into Elizabeth's hand. With her other hand, Ms. Diaz pulls Elizabeth close by the collar.

"Listen to me. Call nine-one-one. Tell them we need an ambulance. Send them to the clearing in the woods. Tell them a student is committing suicide. I'm not sure how."

"What?"

"Call nine-one-one! Do it now!" Ms. Diaz yells and then runs as fast as her legs and heart allow.

CHAPTER 35

"Back from the cordial Grave I drag thee"

Ms. Diaz tears across the partially snow-covered grass. Her body moves instinctively, propelled by adrenaline and fear and a desperate need to defy space and time. *I need to run faster. Go faster. Why do the woods seem so far away?*

Elizabeth stands in shock, watching Ms. Diaz race toward the trees. Did she hear her right? She stares at the cell phone in her hand. When the words register, she dials nine-one-one, presses the phone to her ear, and clears her throat. After a single ring, she starts to panic. *Come on, come on, come on, answer the fucking phone!*

"Nine-one-one. What's your emergency?"

"A student is committing suicide in the woods near the high school. We need an ambulance. Please hurry."

"What's your name?"

"Elizabeth Davis. Please hurry."

"How old are you, Elizabeth?"

"Sixteen. You need to send an ambulance!"

"The ambulance has already been dispatched, Elizabeth. Please stay on the line and try to answer my questions."

"Okay," Elizabeth says shakily. She looks behind her. She's near the door, but if she goes inside, she might lose cell service. *Should I go to the woods, too?* Maybe what she sees will help the operator. She spins around slowly in a circle. No one else is outside. Tears spill down her face.

"Elizabeth, who is in the woods?"

"A student from the high school," she says, choking back tears.

"What's the student's name?"

"I don't know. I just know someone's there."

"How do you know?"

"My teacher told me someone's there and to call nine-one-one. I don't know anything else," Elizabeth says. She tears off her scarf and unzips her jacket. She bends at the waist and puts one hand across her stomach. Whoever is out there is hurt. Maybe screaming and crying for help. Dying. And no one can hear. Elizabeth knows. No one heard when she fell from the tree. She's sobbing, holding the bottom of the phone back to spare the operator her tear-filled, choking sounds.

"You're doing great, Elizabeth. Stay with me."

Elizabeth moves her free hand from her stomach to her mouth in an attempt to trap the noises fighting to get out of her. She looks up and sees Ms. Diaz getting smaller as she moves farther from school and closer to the woods. *I can do this. I have to do this. I'm the only one here. Ms. Diaz is counting on me. Whoever is out there is counting on me.* Elizabeth stands up and wipes her eyes and nose with the back of her hand.

"Are you with me, Elizabeth?" the operator asks.

"I'm here," she says shakily.

"Good. What's your teacher's name?"

"Ms. Diaz. She teaches at the high school. Somehow she knows someone's there. I don't know how."

"Where is your teacher now?"

"She's running into the woods," Elizabeth says as Ms. Diaz disappears into the mass of brown trunks.

Ms. Diaz hops over stumps and clears away branches with her hands. She feels a sting across her cheek, another across her forehead—scratches from branches she couldn't deflect in time. Still, she runs. Her legs pump. Her heart races. Her lungs ache from running in the cold. She runs and prays: *Keep going . . . faster . . . faster . . . Please let me reach her in time . . . Please God, don't take her . . . Not now . . .*

She reaches the clearing, the place where a few trees didn't grow and a person can lie down comfortably. And there she is on her back, her right arm extended, a few inches away from her body, her palm up, her fingers curled. A water bottle lies on its side not far from her hand. Her left arm is closer to her body. She wears jeans tucked into knee-high, white winter boots and a puffy white coat, zipped to the top.

The hood is up, the strings pulled tight, to fight off the cold as she dies.

Ms. Diaz pauses for a second and whispers, "Emily." She races to the girl's side and falls to her knees. She unties the strings and pushes the hood back to get a full look at her face. She's pale but not entirely colorless. Her hair is brushed straight back, pulled into a small ponytail that sits at the base of her neck.

Ms. Diaz bends over, scoops her arm under the girl's shoulders, and lifts her a little. She screams: "Emily! Emily! Wake up! Wake up! Emily! No!"

At the same time, she checks for signs of life: breath, a pulse, a response to the screaming. She unzips the coat halfway and places her hand on Emily's throat. She thinks she can feel a weak throbbing. Emily's eyes are closed. She's not completely cold, not completely warm. There's no blood seeping through her coat or clothes. Death is claiming her from the inside. Ms. Diaz doesn't know how to stop it.

She can only do what she's seen people do on TV and in movies. She isn't sure if it'll help, but it's all she can do. She draws in a deep breath, tilts Emily's head back, pinches her nose, and places her mouth over the girl's. She exhales, pushing air hard into Emily's lungs. Her upper body moves a bit. Ms. Diaz does it again and again and again and again.

Sirens scream in the background, getting louder as they get closer. *They're almost here.* Ms. Diaz continues to breathe into Emily. Feet pound the earth, but it can't be the paramedics yet. Elizabeth races through the trees and into the clearing.

"No, Elizabeth, go back. You shouldn't see this."

"Oh my God," Elizabeth says and covers her mouth.

"Go back!"

Elizabeth kneels on the other side of Emily and takes over breathing into her, not waiting for Ms. Diaz's permission. They take turns. One breathes . . . in and out . . . again and again . . . while the other one prays. *Please, God, let this work.*

They hear voices and boots breaking branches as they tear through the woods. "They're here," Elizabeth says. She stands and yells, "We're over here! We're over here!"

Ms. Diaz hears their voices, but not the individual words. She's focused on breathing . . . in and out . . . again and again. Strong hands easily lift her from under her arms and place her to the side, a few feet away, so the paramedics can get to Emily.

Ms. Diaz rolls on her back and unzips her vest. She massages her throat and chest with one hand and clutches the earth with the other. Her lungs ache and allow only short, rapid breaths. The cool air fuels the burn in her throat and chest. Her head throbs and her heart pounds. She pulls at her turtleneck. She's sweating and wants to rip it off, to stop it from strangling her.

Someone yells, "Are you okay?" After a few times, Ms. Diaz realizes one of the paramedics is talking to her. She nods yes. When he asks, "Are you sure?" she insists, "Yes, I'm fine. Don't worry about me."

Elizabeth kneels next to Ms. Diaz and holds her hand.

Emily is moved this way and that. Her coat is gone and

parts of her white sweater are cut open. There are tubes and bags and needles. At one point, she's rolled on her side so they can slide a board beneath her.

As Emily is turned, she faces Ms. Diaz and Elizabeth. A tube sticks out of her mouth. Strands of hair have escaped from the ponytail and fallen on her pale, bruised cheek. Elizabeth wants to reach out and circle the strands behind the girl's ear. Emily's amber-flecked brown eyes are partially open, but Elizabeth can't tell if they continue to see.

And then, in an instant, she's gone—hoisted in the air and carried away.

In the back of the ambulance, the paramedics work on Emily. Every second matters. They poke and prod her, shine a light in her eyes, and monitor her weak heartbeat. They force air into her lungs and liquid into her veins. They keep in touch with the hospital. When they arrive, Emily is passed to another crew of workers. Her stomach is pumped, but some of the poison has already seeped into her system. Not enough, though. She will survive. Her parents are called. They're on their way.

Time seems to pass at a brutally slow pace as Emily sleeps in a bed in the intensive care unit.

The images in her head are vivid. Are they dreams? Or is this the other side? She's on a plane, the skydiving propeller kind. It glides over the ocean, smoothly at first, but then it hits serious turbulence. She grabs the chair's arms, but this doesn't help to steady her. Nearby is the open area where someone strapped with a parachute would normally jump.

She unlatches her seatbelt and stands. The plane's shaking throws her to the floor. She crawls to the opening and rolls out of the plane.

She falls, twisting through the choppy air, but she never hits the water. The plane circles around and she falls through a hole in the roof. She lands hard on the floor. Everything feels like it's broken. The hole in the ceiling closes and the side opening vanishes. The plane is sealed. No way to escape. The shaking plane drifts from side to side. She crawls back to her seat, fastens her seatbelt, and holds the chair's arms again. She braces herself for the bumpy ride.

No white light. No escorted walk by dead loved ones. She's dreaming, and if she's dreaming, then she must be alive.

Emily pries open her eyes. Her lids are heavy and prefer to remain closed. She blinks several times to clear her vision. She moves only her eyes. Everything else hurts. Her body has been battered by hands and equipment that worked to save her life. She's still attached to some of the machines.

Mamá sits on one side of the bed and holds Emily's hand. Her eyes are closed and her head is lowered. Pop sits on her other side. His elbows press into the bed and his face is buried in his hands. They are praying.

Emily moves her hand to confirm that she's alive and not watching this scene from outside her body. Mamá feels Emily's fingers move. She snaps her head up and leans into her daughter's face.

"Emily? Emily, are you awake?"

Pop also leans in, his face inches from hers.

Emily nods her head weakly. Everything hurts so much.

"*¡Oh, gracias a Dios!*" Mamá exclaims.

Pop runs a hand through his hair and then grips the metal bedrail.

Tears slide out of Emily's closed eyes.

CHAPTER 36

"How well I knew Her not"

Three floors down, Ms. Diaz lies on a bed in the emergency room area with small plastic tubes up her nose and a monitor on her finger.

When she had walked out of the woods, her breathing was still labored.

"Elizabeth," she whispered and faced the girl. Without hesitation, Elizabeth had hugged Ms. Diaz tight. They were both shaking.

"When I first read the note, I thought it was you," said Ms. Diaz.

They had pulled away from each other, but Elizabeth had maintained a grip on Ms. Diaz's arms by the elbows.

"Ms. D? Are you okay? Your face is scratched and you're pale."

Ms. Diaz had touched her cheek where a wayward branch assaulted her. The brush of her fingertips across the scratch had released the tiniest bit of blood. The red speck reminded her of amber flecks in half-closed brown eyes.

She had dropped to her knees. Her upper body felt like it was being squeezed tighter and tighter. She had placed her hands on the ground to steady herself, but it didn't help. Her vision blurred and her chest hurt. She rolled on her back. The earth was cool beneath her; the sun was hot upon her. A strong wind blew over and carried away her consciousness.

Elizabeth had called nine-one-one for a second time.

Now, Ms. Diaz closes her eyes but can't sleep.

After some time, a nurse walks into her room.

"Hey there, sunshine," she says as she reviews Ms. Diaz's chart.

Ms. Diaz laughs a little because she must look like crap. She tries to talk, but her throat is painfully dry.

"Just relax," the nurse says. "I'll get you some water in a minute. The doctor said you don't need to be admitted, but they want you to stay a little longer before you're cleared to go home. He said you probably fainted from a combination of overexertion and anxiety."

Ms. Diaz can't argue with the diagnosis.

"Some of your teacher friends are in the lobby. We won't let them in yet, but one asked me to deliver your bag. She figured you'd need your identification, phone, and whatnot when you woke up."

"Thanks," Ms. Diaz whispers.

"Now, try to get some rest," the nurse says.

Ms. Diaz nods, closes her eyes, and easily falls asleep.

Time passes. At some point, Ms. Diaz opens her eyes and looks around. She's alone. She spots her work bag on a nearby chair and suddenly wonders if the manila envelope is inside.

She slides out of bed and inches her way to the chair, rolling anything that can be rolled and being careful not to detach herself from the machines. When she returns to the bed, she finds and rips open the envelope. She pulls out a marble design–covered journal and begins to read:

Dear Ms. Diaz,

Hi. How are you?

Okay, that was a stupid way to start, but I wasn't sure how to begin. Deep breath and here goes: When you read this, I should be gone. The first envelope is my suicide note, and this journal is the explanation. "This is my letter to the World / That never wrote to Me –" That's a line from an Emily Dickinson poem, but I'm sure you know that. Do you know how that feels? To expect a response from someone and get nothing? She was ignored and resented it. So was I. Not by you. You tried . . .

When she finishes, Ms. Diaz hugs the journal to her chest. She sinks into the bed, turns on her side, and pulls her knees up. Tears stream down her face and into the pillow beneath her head. After a few minutes, the nurse walks into the room.

"The girl who tried to kill herself in the woods, is she alive?" Ms. Diaz asks. She stays rolled away from the nurse, facing the wall.

"I can't give you information about another patient," the nurse says. "That's confidential."

"I found her there. That's why I'm here. I passed out after trying to resuscitate her. Please, I need to know. Is she alive?"

The nurse is quiet for a moment and then she says, "Yes."

Ms. Diaz turns her face into the pillow and sobs.

CHAPTER 37

"Is it too late to touch you, Dear?"

Elizabeth stands alone outside the high school's front entrance. After countless retellings of the morning's events, she's free to go, but where? The principal asked if she wanted to call her mom for a ride home. No. The police offered to give her a ride. Absolutely not. Her mom would have a heart attack. She'd never believe Elizabeth had not been arrested—again. After all, only yesterday the police were involved after she popped Emily in the face.

Yesterday, she hit Emily in the face. Today, she decided to kill herself. And this morning, Elizabeth saw Emily in the distance and decided not to catch up to her. She knows now that Emily was the girl in white walking ahead of her. If Elizabeth had caught up to her, she could have ruined Emily's plan. She saw Emily walking to her death and didn't stop her.

Elizabeth buries her iPod earbuds into her ears, turns the volume way up, and zips up her jacket as high as it'll go. She glances at the nearby wooded area and flashes of Emily on the ground fill her head. Her still eyes. Her cold mouth. Elizabeth's stomach tightens and, without a real destination, she runs away from the school.

After a while, she cuts through the baseball field in Rogers Park. She stops running and turns in a circle. She doesn't want to go home, but she doesn't know where to go.

Her mind races as music pounds in her ears. The sun is high in the clear blue sky, but gusts of cool wind remind her winter isn't over. She throws up her fur-trimmed hood to protect her face against the sun and wind. She glances in one direction. That way leads home. No. She turns in the opposite direction. That way leads back to school. No. She looks to her right and sees a playground. She attacked her father near there. No.

She eyes the town green in the distance and walks through the cemetery to Sophia Holland's grave. She drops her bag on the ground, kneels, and sits back on her heels. She shuts off her iPod but leaves the buds in place. The rushing of her own blood fills her ears, like waves lapping the shore. She shoves her gloved hands into her pockets, tucks her nose under the top of her coat, and closes her eyes.

At first, her body is tense, focused on keeping warm as she kneels on the cold earth. Soon, though, the tension eases as she focuses on her breathing and the darkness behind her eyes. Elizabeth lies down next to Sophia's headstone, her eyes closed, her legs and arms somewhat apart and relaxed, her palms up. Her mind races with questions, apologies, requests for help—from whom she's not sure. But then she hears what seem to be responses, but it's her own voice inside her head.

Elizabeth takes in a deep breath. As she exhales, she imagines releasing her anger and guilt with her breath into the wind. She does it again and imagines that the deep-seated, hard-to-get-to junk seeps through her back and legs into the earth. She does this again and again. The black behind her eyes lightens, and for several minutes, she sees swirls of purple and gold. She wishes she could take a picture of the majestic colors. She holds them as long as she can as she floats for what seems like forever in a semiconscious state.

When Elizabeth opens her eyes, she sees the sun is starting its descent, and the moon is already visible in the sky. The impending sunset brings a deeper chill. Still, she's warm and remarkably relaxed. She props herself on her elbows and looks around.

Some of the grass remains green, while some areas are marred brown by the weather. Some spots are muddy from the melting snow. To the right of her elbow, a thin layer of ice covers a small patch of green grass on Sophia's burial site. She extends her arm and gently presses her palm on the ice, her warm skin turning it into water. The grass is set free to feel the sun's beams and hear the wind's song.

Elizabeth takes her camera out of her bag and rises from the ground. She turns the camera to the north. Click. To the south. Click. To the east. Click. To the west. Click. She points the camera at the sun. Click. And at its cool companion, the moon. Click.

She stares at Sophia's headstone and imagines the letters that spell her name morphing into "Emily Delgado" and then "Emily Elizabeth Davis." A chill shoots through her.

"I'm sorry you died so young," she whispers, "but I'm still alive." Her breath catches in her throat and she swallows hard. "I'll see you on *El Día de los Muertos*. I promise you won't be forgotten, but I can't hang out here anymore."

She picks up her bag and walks off in a new direction.

Elizabeth rings the doorbell, and without waiting for a response, bangs on the door. She knocks continually until Tommy stands at the entrance. The two stare at each other in silence for a few moments.

"Hi," Elizabeth says.

"Hi," Tommy responds, with confusion and surprise in his voice.

She lifts her camera and takes a picture of him.

"Hey," he says, raising a hand like a celebrity ambushed by the paparazzi. "What are you doing?"

"Taking a picture of you."

"I see that. At least warn me or get my good side," he says. He passes a hand over his short hair and strikes a pose. She takes another picture and laughs, which causes Tommy to cock his head and look at her with wonder.

"Can I come in?" Elizabeth asks as she puts the camera into her bag.

"Depends. Are you going to attack me?"

"You never know," she says, raising an eyebrow. When she realizes he's not amused, she adds, "No."

He steps aside and allows Elizabeth to enter.

"Is anyone home?" she asks, unzipping her coat.

"Just me. Come on in. Have a seat," he says as he walks toward the nearby living room.

"No thanks, I'm not staying long," she says. She shoves her gloves into her coat pockets and lowers her bag to the floor.

Tommy sits on an arm of the couch, while Elizabeth stands a few feet away.

"I need to tell and ask you something."

"All right," says Tommy. He crosses his arms and looks at her with interest and suspicion.

She shifts from one foot to the other before saying, "I'm really sorry."

"It's okay," he says, waving her off. "I deserved it. I shouldn't have trusted Kevin to be a reliable reporter of information. I should have known better after being his friend all these years. I should have asked you myself."

"Yeah, but you didn't deserve what I did to you. I'm really sorry. For everything. I'm going to work on, you know, not losing it anymore," she says and grins.

"It's nice to see you smile," says Tommy.

Elizabeth bites her bottom lip.

"So, what do you want to ask?" Tommy reminds her.

Elizabeth steps toward him. She nibbles on a fingernail and then steps closer. In response, Tommy unlocks his crossed arms and widens his legs so nothing blocks her from reaching him. She leans in and outlines Tommy's earlobe with her nose. She gently kisses him on his neck, below his ear. "Am I too late?"

He pulls off Elizabeth's jacket and wraps his arms around her back. She circles her arms around his neck and holds on tight. Tommy's hands seem to inject warmth into her body. Elizabeth pulls back so her face is next to Tommy's. He leans back a little farther and turns his face to kiss her. His lips brush hers, once, twice. Then, he extends the kiss and opens his lips a bit. Elizabeth responds, and after a few kisses, she lets him in.

His hands grab her back and pull her into him. She grips his shoulder with one hand and reaches up with the other to rub the back of his head, his buzz cut soft beneath her fingers. Her eyes are shut tight, and for a moment she sees tinges of purple and gold again.

They pause. She keeps her head near his and they continue to hold each other.

"Wow," says Elizabeth.

"Yeah," says Tommy.

"Don't let go. I feel a little dizzy," she says and laughs.

"Well, that's typical when you experience what I like to call the Ultimate Tommy Tongue Twister," he says.

"Don't be gross," Elizabeth giggles. "You'll ruin the moment."

"*Lo siento, querida,*" says Tommy. "I'll be quiet, and I won't let go. I promise."

They hold each other gently; the tips of his fingers draw small circles on her back, and her hand strokes his chest. Elizabeth turns her head and sees rays of the setting sun stream through the living room window.

"I have to go," she says.

"What? You just told me not to let go, so you're trapped here forever," he says. He locks his legs behind her and tickles her with his hands.

Elizabeth squirms and laughs for a few moments. She kisses him on the lips and says, "I really do need to leave."

Tommy brushes a thumb across her lips and kisses her again. Elizabeth picks up her jacket and bag and holds Tommy's hand as they walk to the front door. She turns and kisses him again.

"Talk to you later," she says and then walks toward home.

Elizabeth stands outside her house for a while, looking at the front door like she's a traveler unsure if she's reached her destination. She hesitates because the conversation she plans to have with her mom will be their first real talk in months.

"Hello? Mom? Lily?" Elizabeth closes the door behind her. She unzips her coat, shoves her gloves into her pockets, and drops her bag by the coatrack.

Lily races around a corner and skids to a stop when she sees Elizabeth. Her mom is right behind Lily. Her eyes are puffy like she's been crying.

"Elizabeth!" Lily screams. She runs to her sister and hugs her. Her mom stares at Elizabeth and walks slowly toward her. She wraps her arms around Elizabeth's neck and holds her tight.

Elizabeth doesn't know why they're hugging her, but she doesn't say anything or pull away. She wraps an arm around her mom's waist and places her other hand on the top of Lily's head. She's holding her breath, and when she finally exhales, she begins to sob. They all hold each other tighter.

After a while, Elizabeth stops crying and begins to breathe normally. The three pull apart, and her mom wipes Elizabeth's face and kisses her on the cheek. Elizabeth stares at her mother with wide eyes. Her mother kisses her again and says, "We were so worried about you. Come on, take your coat off and let's sit down and talk."

Elizabeth's mom helps her out of her coat and hangs it on a hook. She holds Elizabeth's hand and leads her into the living room. Lily trails behind them. Elizabeth and her mom sit on the couch and Lily hops onto a nearby chair. Elizabeth sits next to her mom but holds a pillow in front of her chest like a shield. Her mom reaches out and strokes the side of Elizabeth's head. She pulls her head slightly in the other direction. Her mother notices the subtle movement and pulls her hand back.

"Why were you so worried about me?" Elizabeth asks.

"Because of what happened this morning," her mom said. "Ms. Gilbert called to see if you were okay, and I told her you never came home from detention. Of course, I panicked and asked her why you wouldn't be okay. She told me what happened and she said you had left school hours ago."

"I did," Elizabeth says.

"Right, so when you didn't come home, I began to worry. After what you saw this morning . . . I can't even imagine seeing that girl lying there half-dead . . ."

"Her name's Emily," Elizabeth says.

"Emily," her mom repeats. "That poor girl . . . and her family."

"Is she dead?" Elizabeth asks. She grasps the pillow tighter, her nails buried into the foam. "Did Ms. Gilbert say if she's alive or . . ."

"She's alive," her mother says. Elizabeth releases her grip on the pillow. "Ms. Gilbert said she's still in the hospital, but she's alive. I was feeling so sorry for her family, and then you didn't come home, and I was so worried we would become that family. I had no idea where you were. I tried calling you on your cell phone."

"You have my cell phone," Elizabeth says.

"Yes, I remembered when it rang in my dresser drawer."

Elizabeth and Lily look at each other and laugh.

"This isn't funny," says their mom. "I was worried sick. We drove around town for a while . . ."

"For a while?" asks Lily. "It was like forever." She rolls her eyes.

"What, did you have something better to do?" Elizabeth asks, teasing her sister.

"Would you two please stop? This is serious."

"Sorry," says Lily. As soon as her mom turns to continue talking, Lily sticks her tongue out at Elizabeth, who winks back.

"Anyway, we drove around, but I ran out of places to check," says her mom. "I had no idea where to find you." Her mom starts to cry. Elizabeth and Lily stop smirking.

"And what if you were hurt someplace, like Emily, and you needed my help, and I had no idea where to find you?" She pauses and wipes her eyes. "I'm your mom, and I should know where you hang out. What if you were hurt? What if you needed me? I couldn't find you, Elizabeth. I couldn't find you."

"Mom, I'm not hurt," says Elizabeth. She lowers her pillow-shield a little. "I'm sorry. I should have come straight home, but I needed to think."

Her mom reaches out, squeezes Elizabeth's hand, and lets go. "You don't need to apologize, baby. I'm the one who's sorry. I've been a wreck since your father left. I know that." She starts to cry again. "I wasn't a good enough wife, so I lost your father, and then I was a lousy mom, so I lost you, too."

"I'm right here," says Elizabeth. She sets the pillow aside and moves closer to her mom. She holds her hand. "You haven't lost me. I'm right here. You're not a lousy mom."

"Things are going to change." She wipes her eyes again and strokes Elizabeth's hair. Elizabeth doesn't move this time. "I want to know all about your friends and why you dye your hair and cut classes and punch people out."

They all laugh.

"Really, I want to know why instead of yelling at you or turning my head and pretending like it's not happening."

"Denial ain't just a river in Egypt," says Lily.

They laugh again.

"Where did you hear that?" Elizabeth asks.

"School," says Lily. "I can't remember who said it or why, but it sounded funny."

"Anyway," her mom continues. "I want to know. I want you to talk to me."

"Okay," says Elizabeth. "I'm going to try to be better, too . . . ," she says, hesitating. "And Mom? I was thinking about calling Dad tomorrow and seeing if he'll talk to me."

"Of course he'll talk to you, baby. He loves you," her mom says.

Elizabeth flinches at her words and shakes her head.

"He loves you, Elizabeth, like I do," her mom says.

Elizabeth bows her head and continues to shake her head in disbelief.

"I love you, Elizabeth," her mother says. She puts a finger under Elizabeth's chin and raises her head. "Look at me, sweetie. I love you so much, you have no idea. I'm sorry you haven't felt that. I'll say it a thousand times a day until you believe me."

"I love you, too," says Lily. She jumps off the chair and hops onto the couch behind Elizabeth. She leans into her sister. Tears stream down Elizabeth's face. Her mother brushes them away with her hands.

"Boy, we're a mess, huh?" her mom says.

Her mom's dark circles are there, as usual, and her eyes are rimmed red from crying, but her pale-green eyes radiate certainty and confidence.

"Hold on a second," says Elizabeth. She stands and walks out of the room. She returns to the living room with her camera and sits between her mother and sister.

"Everyone squeeze together," says Elizabeth.

"Whose is that?" asks her mother.

"It's from school."

"Do they know you have it?"

Elizabeth stares at her. "Yes, Julia, I use the camera for the school newspaper. I didn't steal it."

"That's great, but if you did steal it, we'd discuss it as a family."

"Yeah, yeah, just move in closer," says Elizabeth.

"You want to take a picture now? Oh, honey, we look awful."

"No, we don't," says Elizabeth. "We look beautiful. Tears and all. Come on. Move in close."

The three squish together. Lily smiles wide and says an extended, "Cheeeeeese." Elizabeth stretches out her arms and turns the camera toward them. When she's about to take the picture, her mom kisses Elizabeth on her forehead. Elizabeth closes her eyes and smiles.

Click.

Suddenly, Elizabeth's exhausted. Her mom and sister are beat, too. It's not that late, but they all decide to get into pajamas. After Lily changes clothes, she crawls into Elizabeth's bed.

"Hey, what are you doing?" asks Elizabeth as she brushes her hair by her dresser.

"Let's end the night with a slumber party," says Lily. She pats the covers next to her. "Come on."

Elizabeth smiles. "Fine. I won't kick you out."

Her mom stands in the doorway to see what's going on.

Lily pats the bed again. "Come on, Mom, we're having a slumber party."

Her mom looks at Elizabeth. "Come on," says Elizabeth.

"All right," her mom says. "Move over, Rover."

Lily giggles and creates room for everyone. Elizabeth climbs in, followed by her mom. Lily jumps out of bed and returns with three stuffed animals, one for each of them. As they settle into bed, Elizabeth's mother softly sings a lullaby, like she used to do during thunderstorms. Tonight, though, everything is clear and calm. After a few minutes of listening to her mother's soothing song, Elizabeth, for the first time in over a year, falls into a deep, restful sleep.

CHAPTER 38

"Such are the inlets of the mind -"

Everything in Emily's hospital room is plastic with no sharp edges, and everything is monitored: blood pressure, heart rate, temperature, eating, going to the bathroom, medication. She takes her pills. They check her mouth to confirm she swallows them. Other things drip directly into her blood through the IV.

She's never alone.

She wants to be left alone.

They ask her countless questions.

She doesn't answer any of them.

They can't help her if she doesn't talk to them.

On day four, she starts to feel better physically, but she's angry and embarrassed. Her parents and brother are constant visitors. This doesn't help. A small group of interns marches in. This doesn't help, either. Here, young doctors, this is what a suicide survivor looks like. Interesting, isn't it? Here are her charts, take a peek. Go ahead, take notes, but don't tap the glass. Let's not irritate her further.

One day, her parents are out of the room when a psychiatrist or psychologist or social worker comes in. Different person, same questions. This time, Emily answers a select few.

"What would I have done differently that day? I would've written DNR on my chest with a black permanent marker."

"Do Not Resuscitate?" he asks, peering over his glasses.

"Good point. I would've written it out to prevent any misunderstanding," Emily says. "And, what would I say to Ms. Diaz or Elizabeth if they were here right now? I'd say, 'Fuck you.'"

"But if they didn't find you, you'd be dead."

"Exactly."

The doctor scribbles furiously. Emily's comments win her more days in the hospital. This is fine with her. The alternative is going home, and once she goes home, they may want her to go back to school. No way.

On day six, Emily feels better overall. She's hydrated, medicated, and well nourished. The sight of her parents doesn't trigger a desire to puke or throw something.

Pop reads to her from the newspaper at first, but then switches to a lighthearted novel since the news is always tragic. She doesn't tell him that she's already read the book.

Mamá's more clearheaded than usual. She pushes her daughter's hair away from her face like she did when Emily was young and didn't feel well. Mamá was never very affectionate, but Emily remembers this—how Mamá pushed aside her hair and checked for a fever with the back of her hand.

Austin entertains her with his college stories and promises to visit on the weekends more often. He tells her Kevin came to the hospital, but the nurses said immediate family only. He delivers a postcard from Kevin to Emily that says, "Wish you were here." Austin doesn't ever mention Abby and bolts out of the room when he feels like crying.

The monster inside her is weakened, but not dead. The medical team tries to pull it out of her, but she doesn't cooperate. She won't talk. She answers some of their questions, but she won't open up.

Still, they say talking even a little is progress. They push her a bit. They ask her to help create a safety plan and sign a no-suicide contract.

She won't make any promises.

This means more days in the hospital.

CHAPTER 39

"Growth of Man – like Growth of Nature –"

Ms. Diaz stands in front of her period one class for the first time since Emily's attempted suicide and her own five-day medical leave. She can't ignore what happened, but she doesn't want to dwell on it, either. The students sit in their seats silently and wait for her to say something.

Kevin's face is ashen. Tommy stares at the floor and Abby and Sarah turn away whenever Ms. Diaz glances at them. Elizabeth sits up straight and looks directly at her teacher.

"Hi," Ms. Diaz says finally.

The students laugh a little.

"A while ago, a student asked me why I became a teacher," Ms. Diaz says and glances at Elizabeth. "I said I teach because I love literature. She pointed out I didn't say anything about my students. What happened with Emily made me realize

I do love my students. And since I have the news editor in the room, let me clarify that I do not love any of you in an inappropriate way. Got that, Mr. Bowles?"

"Got it," Tommy says.

"What I mean is I don't only care about whether you can read and write well. I care about you as people, and I believe you are capable of great things. Each of you will contribute something to this world. You are important. You would be missed."

Ms. Diaz closes her eyes for a few moments, then opens them and says:

All but Death, can be Adjusted –
Dynasties repaired –
Systems – settled in their Sockets –
Citadels – dissolved –

Wastes of Lives – resown with Colors
By Succeeding Springs –
Death – unto itself – Exception –
Is exempt from Change –

Ms. Diaz lets her words sink in. She looks at each of them and smiles kindly. She stops when she gets to Emily's empty seat.

Everyone is still for a few moments and then Ms. Diaz says, "Let's get back to work."

Students groan.

At the end of class, Elizabeth asks Ms. Diaz, "Can I come see you at lunch?"

"Sure. Are you okay?"

"I'm fine. Really. I want to open my shoe box."

Ms. Diaz's eyes widen. "Yeah?"

"I'm ready," says Elizabeth. "Are you?"

"I'm ready. I'll see you at lunch."

Elizabeth meets Tommy at the door and slips her hand into his as they walk away.

At lunchtime, Elizabeth comes alone and pulls a chair close to her teacher's desk. Ms. Diaz hands Elizabeth the shoe box and sets her binder directly in front of her.

"Ready?" Ms. Diaz asks.

"Ready," says Elizabeth. "On the count of three."

"Sure," Ms. Diaz says and laughs. On three, they rip off the tape. Ms. Diaz opens the binder and Elizabeth takes off the shoe box lid. They're quiet and alternately look at each other and the contents. Ms. Diaz flips the pages of the binder and unfolds some pages that were shoved inside. Elizabeth takes out her drawings, pictures, and poems, one by one.

"Some of these are pretty bad," Elizabeth says and laughs.

"I'm sure some are pretty good, too," says Ms. Diaz.

They continue to examine their work. Elizabeth opens her lunch bag and pulls out a sandwich, a bag of chips, an apple, and a soda.

"Apple for the teacher?" she asks.

"Thanks," Ms. Diaz says and smiles. "So, how are you, really?"

"I'm okay. My mom packed me a lunch and drove me to school today, and I talked to my dad a little bit."

"That's great. And, there's Tommy."

"Yeah," says Elizabeth, smiling. "What about you? Are you okay?"

"I'm not sure, but I know I need to move forward with my life, which includes doing something with this. It's not going to be easy, but I'm ready."

"What are you going to do with it?" asks Elizabeth.

"Not sure yet. What about you?"

"I might enter the art show," says Elizabeth. "I want to combine the poems with the pictures and drawings. A lot will have to be revised and redrawn. Most of these were done quickly. Will you help me with the poems?"

"I'd love to," says Ms. Diaz. "You're going to display your work? That's a big step."

"Yeah, but I think I'm ready. Maybe these will be my contribution to the world."

"I'm sure you'll contribute to the world in many ways, Elizabeth."

"Do you think she'll come back to school this year?" asks Elizabeth.

"No. Ms. Gilbert said she'll probably have a tutor from the homebound program through the end of the school year. If she's ready, she'll return in September."

"I want to tell her how sorry I am," says Elizabeth.

"You can write to her or you can wait and focus on yourself for a bit. You've been through a lot, too."

"You, too," says Elizabeth.

For the rest of the period, they nibble on their lunches and quietly sort through the fragments of their lives spread out before them.

CHAPTER 40

"I found the words to every thought"

MARCH 15

On day eight, Emily feels stronger, lighter. She talks more to the doctors who stream in and out of her room. She's making progress, they tell her. She knows. She can feel it. The monster is wounded but still breathes. She has more work to do. She won't be able to walk away and leave all the psychiatrists and psychologists and social workers behind. She knows there'll be more of the same after she's discharged. She's beginning to accept this and the idea of home, but not school. She will not go back to school this year. That's fine, they say. We'll make other arrangements.

Still, Emily is apprehensive about leaving. She first saw the hospital as a prison. Now it's more of a cozy sanctuary. Everything runs on routines. Everything is monitored, and if something is "off," it's adjusted to what's considered "normal."

What happens when she goes home? Will everything start to unravel again? One thing she's learned from her chats with the shrinks is that she can't control what others think or do. She can only control her own thoughts, actions, and emotions. So, the big question hanging above her head is: How will she respond to her family and friends and Kevin and school once she's out of the hospital?

Emily doesn't know the answer. She doesn't know if she's strong enough to navigate her life and not lose herself again. Some days she thinks she is. Other days, she's not sure.

Emily stands by the window and watches the sky pelt the earth with a rainstorm designed to erase winter and make room for spring. Just then, a nurse walks in with an envelope.

"What's this?" Emily asks.

"You've got mail," she says.

She opens the envelope and pulls out the card that has a sketch on the front of three people making snow angels. Emily recognizes the artist's style. Inside the card is a photograph of Elizabeth, Tommy, Kevin, and Lily, all making silly faces, and a handwritten note:

Dear Emily,

Ms. Diaz's favorite female recluse once wrote: "The soul selects her own society –" Right now, you may hate us, and I know we're a bunch of crazy misfits, but we're so very sorry and we miss you. When you come home, if it makes you feel better, you can punch us each in the face (except

*for Lily) because we deserve it. After that, maybe
we can go bowling and cream the boys again. It
can be a real double date this time. I guess what
I'm trying to say is, you're not alone, and we hope
when you come home you'll select us as your
society.*

   Peace,

   Elizabeth

Emily holds the card to her chest and sinks to the floor. She opens her mouth and lets out a wail. Nurses fly into her room and surround her, checking if she hurt herself. They lift her off the floor and walk her to the bed. Emily climbs in, hugs her pillow, and sobs uncontrollably. People are called. Coded language is used.

The doctor arrives and asks new questions, ones that assess whether she knows what's real. Is she seeing things? Hearing voices? Emily realizes they think she's much worse and losing touch with reality. She forces herself to sit up and gain control of her crying. She hands the card to the doctor. He has been here before, asking her questions about her family and friends. He reads the card and looks at Emily.

"Is this why you're crying?"

"Yes," she whispers. Tears spill down her cheeks.

"Do you want to talk?"

Emily nods.

The doctor sighs with relief and dismisses the nurses. He listens and takes notes and asks a few questions, but Emily does most of the talking. She talks about bowling and snow angels and catching flakes on her tongue. About sharing Pop-Tarts with an unlikely friend and finally kissing the boy she's liked since the second grade. She talks about Austin teaching her to play dominoes and Pop running beside her when she learned to ride a bike. She describes Mamá's laughter and how she misses hearing it.

For the first time, she talks about love and needing people and wanting to be strong all the time, not only sometimes. Even if she's wounded, she will never give up. She'll create a safety plan. Whatever they want, she'll do it. It won't be easy, but right now, on day eight, something has clicked inside of her. The monster is in a half nelson hold and she won't let go.

"I want to go home," she says.

CHAPTER 41

" 'Hope' is the thing
with feathers –"

MAY 15

Two months pass. Snow stops falling and the wind loses its brutal bite. The days get warmer, and the sky often cries to soften the earth's surface and feed the flowers eager to decorate the world.

Ms. Diaz strolls into the main office before her first period class to check her mailbox. She recycles most of the contents, as usual, but among the junk is an envelope addressed to her in actual handwriting. She checks the return address and stands frozen for a moment before returning to her classroom. After period one, she asks Elizabeth, Tommy, and Kevin to see her at lunchtime. "Bring your jackets," she tells them.

When they arrive, Ms. Diaz shoves the letter into her pocket, puts on her coat, and leads them outside.

"Where are we going?" asks Elizabeth.

"To the woods."

Elizabeth and the boys stop in their tracks, but Ms. Diaz walks on.

"Ms. D! Hey! Stop!" Elizabeth shouts. They run to catch up. Elizabeth stands in front of Ms. Diaz to stop her. Tommy and Kevin stand to the side.

"Ms. D, what are you doing? Why are you going to the woods?" Elizabeth asks.

"Emily wrote me a letter."

"Really?" asks Elizabeth, her eyes open wide.

"Yes, it's in my pocket."

"Okay, but why go there? I don't think it's a good idea. Back me up here, guys," she says.

"Definitely a bad idea," says Tommy.

Kevin stares at the ground and snorts back a sniffle. "I can't, Ms. D," he says softly.

"We need to," she says and places a hand on Kevin's shoulder. "Before what happened, it was one of my favorite places. I brought my students there each year to write poetry. I can't imagine never going back. I need to reclaim the space, to see it as a stunning display of nature, not a mausoleum."

"Fine," says Elizabeth. "That's your thing. We don't need to go."

Tommy crosses his arms. Kevin clasps his hands behind his head and walks in tight circles. Elizabeth closes her eyes for a moment. Tommy steps closer and holds her hand.

"I could use the company," Ms. Diaz says. "I figure there's

strength in numbers. It might be easier if we go together. We don't have much time. Will you come with me?"

Elizabeth sighs and shifts from one foot to the other. Kevin and Tommy nod. "Fine," says Elizabeth. "Let's go."

The four walk side by side to the woods' entrance, where Ms. Diaz takes the lead and walks without haste. She carefully pulls aside or steps over any branches in their way. She turns around often to make sure the others notice the obstacles.

They walk past the area where Elizabeth fell. They continue deep into the trees to reach the clearing.

Tommy leaps atop a downed tree trunk and walks across it. Kevin walks the area's perimeter. He looks down and sees remnants of autumn and winter. Layers of dried-up leaves, buried for months by ice and snow, cake the ground. Ms. Diaz pats him on the shoulder as she strolls by. The branches above her sprout new life—young, strong, green leaves that hold on tight as the spring wind whistles through them. The sun shines almost directly above them in the clear blue sky.

Elizabeth inches toward the area in the center, the small clearing where a few trees didn't grow. She stares at the spot where Emily swallowed a handful of pills.

Ms. Diaz calls to Tommy and Kevin and moves toward Elizabeth. She stands next to her and looks down, too.

"Let's sit," she says.

Elizabeth snaps her head up. "Right here? Seriously?"

Ms. Diaz lowers herself to the ground and crosses her legs beneath her. She plucks a nearby dandelion and tucks it behind her ear.

Kevin and Tommy sit opposite Ms. Diaz. Tommy gently tugs Elizabeth's hand, inviting her to join them. She sits in front of him, inside the "V" of his legs, and leans back into him. Tommy rests his chin on her shoulder.

Ms. Diaz rips open the envelope and removes the letter. "Do you want to hear it?" she asks.

"Yes," Kevin and Tommy say at once.

"No," says Elizabeth. "I mean, she wrote it to you. You should read it first."

Ms. Diaz reads the letter silently.

Dear Ms. Diaz,

I've been home for two months after being in the hospital for a little while. I can't get into that right now. I don't have enough time or paper. I won't be coming back to school this year. I was going to write sooner, but I wasn't ready. Even now, I'm stumbling over my thoughts, so I'm just going to spit it out: I'm sorry for choosing you to find me. It wasn't fair to do that to you. I also want to say thank you for finding me in time. I know Elizabeth was there, too. Please thank her for me. I have so much more to say, but I can't right now. My mind and hand freeze up whenever I try to get it out.

The one thing that keeps popping into my head is a dream I had recently. I know you'll understand it since you read my journal.

I was on a plane, the skydiving propeller kind. It

glided over the ocean. The nose started to dip. I wasn't
sure if it was going to crash or not, and I didn't want
to wait to find out. The side door was open, and no one
else was aboard. I walked to the edge and dived into
the ocean like an Olympian.

The ascent toward the bright light above the
surface was easy since I pushed hard with my arms
and kicked my legs. I broke through the water's
surface and inhaled the fresh air. I flipped on my back
and floated, surrendering to the push and pull of the
waves. The water moved me gently, here and there,
while the sun warmed my face. I closed my eyes and
smiled. When I woke up, I was still smiling.

I'm okay . . . not great . . . not yet, but I'm
getting better. I want to get better. I wanted you to
know that.

Love,

Emily

P.S. Please tell Elizabeth, Kevin, and Tommy not to
feel guilty. What I did wasn't their fault.

P.S.S. Tell them, too, that I choose them as my
society. They'll understand.

"She forgives you for hitting her," says Ms. Diaz.

Elizabeth covers her mouth with her hand. Tommy holds
her tighter.

"She says none of you are responsible for what she did, and
she chooses you as her society."

They all smile at each other.

"So, is she okay?" Elizabeth asks.

"She says she's okay . . . not great . . . not yet."

"Not *yet*," says Elizabeth.

She looks at a small bush nearby covered with buds. Like a zoom lens, her eyes zero in on one that's green, tight, and closed off on one side. On the other side, small white petals push their way into the world. With a little more sun and water, the bud will bloom.

"So, there's hope," Elizabeth concludes. She squeezes Tommy's hands and considers Kevin's tears and the dandelion peeking through Ms. Diaz's hair. Elizabeth nods and says, "There's always hope."

Emily sits in the oversize chair in front of her window, knees pulled to her chest, hugged by thin arms. Sunlight flickers through the trees' waving branches. She closes her eyes and holds them there for a moment, like she's taking a mental picture, and then rises from her chair and moves to her desk.

She pins a picture on the new corkboard that hangs on the wall above her desk. She had ripped down the old one when she first came home. Most of the pictures were of her, Abby, and Sarah. On her new corkboard, she displays one picture of the three of them—her favorite one. She stands between Abby and Sarah, arms wrapped around their shoulders. Abby flashes a peace sign, and Sarah leans her head against Emily's.

She has a wide, genuine smile on her face. They all do. Emily's working her way back to being that girl.

She pins up other things, too: the picture and card Elizabeth sent her and her safety plan, a signed promise to take any prescribed medication, remain in counseling, and tell someone if she ever feels hopeless again. She won't keep the plan hidden in a drawer; she wants it to stare her in the face.

Emily sits at her desk and opens a new journal with a marble-design cover. She writes out two phrases from Emily Dickinson poems in large, black letters so she can see them easily from anywhere in the room. Turns out, Dickinson also wrote a lot about life and beauty and joy and love. These are the poems she reads now. She rips the pages out of her journal and pins them to the corkboard.

She walks across the room to see if the letters are large enough to read from a distance. She reads the first one out loud: "Unable are the Loved to die / For Love is Immortality, . . ." She reads it again and again. She lets it sink in.

She reads the other quote: "Live – Aloud!"

She repeats it:

Live – Aloud!

Live. Aloud.

Live.

Live.

Live.

Author's Note

Unfortunately, suicide is the third leading cause of death among US adolescents, and Latina teens are at an increased risk for depression, thoughts of suicide, and suicide attempts. If you or anyone you know is struggling with depression or having suicidal thoughts, please seek help. You are important. You would be missed.

National Suicide Prevention Lifeline: 1-800-273-8255
National Hopeline Network: 1-800-442-4673

The characters in *When Reason Breaks* represent pieces of the iconic American poet Emily Dickinson. My hope is that this story is compelling regardless of the reader's knowledge of

Dickinson. At the same time, I hope it sparks an interest in teens to explore Dickinson's life and work.

My own interest in and knowledge of Dickinson developed during an author-centered graduate class at Central Connecticut State University. While writing this novel, I often returned to Cynthia Griffin Wolff's *Emily Dickinson* and the Emily Dickinson Museum website for information. Here are the connections between Dickinson and the novel.

Emily Elizabeth Dickinson was a middle child born on December 10, 1830. Her older brother was William Austin Dickinson, and her younger sister was Lavinia Norcross Dickinson. Their father was an attorney and politician who served in the Massachusetts legislature and as a Whig in the Thirty-third Congress. A stern conservative, he traveled often but, when home, his word ruled. Dickinson loved and respected her father immensely but frequently felt ignored or underestimated by him. She had a strained relationship with her mother, who was often emotionally distant and physically ill.

Dickinson was an intellectual who had a sharp wit and great passion for her work as a poet, having written close to 1,800 poems. Only ten of her poems were published during her lifetime, probably without her knowledge. Along with her poetry, Dickinson is famous for her reclusive lifestyle in her later years; even then, though, she maintained ties with a tight circle of friends and family. An avid reader and letter writer, she was a fan of Shakespeare and Thoreau, and the Brontës were her literary contemporaries. She was an artist, a keen observer of her surroundings, and a lover of nature who often pondered life, death, and immortality.

Emily, Elizabeth, and Ms. Diaz share Dickinson's first name and initials. Emily Delgado's father is a lawyer and politician and her mother is detached and ailing. She has an older brother, Austin, who attends Amherst College. Like Dickinson, Emily Delgado initially has a normal social life as a young person, including crushes, but ultimately pulls away from most of her friends. Emily Delgado writes the letters to Ms. Diaz and reads Thoreau as an escape at the party. In the end, her need for space and privacy causes her to retreat from her society, and her written work—her journal—is found after her attempted suicide. There is evidence that Dickinson experienced depression, but none that she was suicidal; this is particular to Emily Delgado as a character. Emily Delgado wears white in the clearing. Dickinson was buried in white.

Elizabeth represents Dickinson's darker, bolder poems. Many have an angry tone and some are Gothic. Like Dickinson, Elizabeth is a poet and a visual artist. Elizabeth's poem is published in the student newspaper without her approval; it is written in the 8/6/8/6 syllable pattern often used by Dickinson. During the novel, Elizabeth reads *Wuthering Heights* by Emily Brontë and *Jane Eyre* by Charlotte Brontë. Elizabeth is fascinated by the local cemetery and the gravesite of Sophia Holland, in particular. Emily Dickinson was distraught when her cousin and friend Sophia Holland died at a young age. Elizabeth's sister Lily represents Dickinson's younger sister, Lavinia, and her father's affair represents the famous affair between Dickinson's brother, Austin, and Mabel Loomis Todd, both of whom were married.

Ms. Diaz is an intellectual and a writer who reveres nature as Dickinson did. She's passionate about her work and adorns her classroom with posters of Shakespeare and Thoreau, two of Dickinson's favorites.

Tommy Bowles represents two important men in Dickinson's life: Thomas Wentworth Higginson and Samuel Bowles. Higginson was a mentor to Dickinson and coeditor of the first two collections of her poems. Bowles was the owner and editor in chief of the *Springfield Republican* and a close friend. Of the poems that were published in her lifetime, five were published in the *Springfield Republican*. Some scholars argue Dickinson may have had a romantic interest in both Higginson and Bowles.

Suzanne Gilbert, the guidance counselor, represents Susan Huntington Gilbert Dickinson, Emily's sister-in-law and long-time friend. Their relationship was at times loving, and at times contentious.

Some researchers say Dickinson was upset when Susan started to date Austin. Also, her letters to her female friends were so intense that scholars question if she had romantic feelings for any of them, Susan Gilbert in particular. This is represented by Emily's reaction to Abby's relationship with her brother and the suggestions that she might be attracted to Abby or the freshman, Sue Huntington. Two of Dickinson's close childhood friends were named Sarah Tracy and Abby Wood.

I continue to admire Dickinson's life and work. Like others, I am grateful that her brilliant words were found and published, making the poet and her work immortal and poem #1212 ring true:

A word is dead
When it is said,
Some say.

I say it just
Begins to live
That day.

Acknowledgments

I am grateful to everyone who helped to turn my ideas and dreams into reality. Thank you to my awesome agent, Laura Langlie, for taking a chance on me and for being so supportive and persistent. Thanks to my editor, Mary Kate Castellani, and everyone at Bloomsbury USA Children's who helped to bring *When Reason Breaks* to life. Mary Kate, your brilliant comments and insights helped to shape this story into its best possible version. A huge thanks to my family and friends for all their love and support. You were always willing to babysit, read drafts, offer words of encouragement, and whatever else I needed. I couldn't have done this without you: Mom, Dad, Tía Mercia, Marcel, Mimi, Niko, Tyler, Saryna, Dean, Alyna, Evan, Melody Moore, Matt Eagan, my Glastonbury critique group, and all my friends and colleagues in West

Hartford and online. A special thanks to Dr. Melissa Mentzer from Central Connecticut State University for introducing me to Emily Dickinson's poetry, and to Dr. Katherine Sugg for encouraging and supporting me as a writer during and since graduate school. Thank you to Kimberly Sabatini, who introduced me to a great group of people at my first SCBWI conference, and thanks to my new writer friends from the Fearless Fifteeners, the Class of 2K15, and Latin@s in Kid Lit. Finally, thank you to my daughter, Maria Luisa, for putting up with me throughout this process. I love you and I hope Mommy makes you proud!